NEW MAPS

deindustrial fiction

VOL. 3, NO. 1
WINTER 2023

LOOSELEAF PUBLISHING

Bayfield, Wisconsin

About New Maps

New Maps publishes stories in the growing genre of deindustrial fiction, which explores the long decline of industrial civilization, its aftermath, and the new worlds made possible by its departure. The magazine also publishes essays, book reviews, letters to the editor, and other content that examines these themes. For more on the philosophy of the magazine, see the website below, or get acquainted by way of this issue.

Submissions of any of the foregoing may be addressed to the editor at either of the addresses below. Story submission guidelines may be found on the website or requested by post.

New Maps is published quarterly by Looseleaf Publishing. Subscriptions are currently available in the U.S., Australia, Belgium, Canada, Germany, Hong Kong, Ireland, Japan, the Netherlands, New Zealand, Sweden, Taiwan, and the U.K. An annual subscription is $48.00 USD for U.S. addresses, with different prices elsewhere, and may be purchased from the website below, or by writing to request an order form.

Postal correspondence:
Looseleaf Publishing
87095 Valley Road
Bayfield, WI 54814, USA

Online:
www.new-maps.com
editor@new-maps.com

ISSN: 2767-388X

Copyright © February 2023 by Looseleaf Publishing. All stories and essays in this magazine are copyrighted by their respective authors and used here with permission. All rights reserved.

Image credits:
— Cover art © 2023 by Nathan B. Peltier.
— Book covers on p. 16 © 2017 and 2018, respectively, by Harper Voyager.
— Book cover on p. 20 © 2014 HarperCollins.

The stories contained herein are works of fiction. All characters and events portrayed in the stories in this publication are fictional, and any semblance to real people or events is purely coincidental.

Contents

Introduction to the Magic Issue iv
Letters 1

Essays & Sundries   5
Cheap Thrills: Legend Tripping 7
Book Reviews 16
Two Haiku 23

Stories   25

Justin Patrick Moore
A Rat in the Cell 27

David Crawford
Way Out 38

Eric Rust Backos
True Math 59

G. Kay Bishop
Kedorra's Kin 68

Santiago De Choch
The Goddess of Immokalee 75

About This Issue   106
Contributors 106
Colophon & Acknowledgments 108

Introduction to the Magic Issue

The roots of this issue go back to the early days of *New Maps*: not long after I released the first issue in early 2021, I received an unusual submission: an epic, action-filled story set in what was clearly a deindustrial Florida, but suffused quite openly with powerful magic.

Now, from the beginning of *New Maps*, I've never considered magic something that disqualifies a story. This magazine exists to explore the kinds of futures that will arrive in the real world, which means I've had to disqualify stories featuring ideas that, to those committed to the shopworn mythos of endless progress, seem like likely fixtures of our future—extraplanetary colonization, for example, is accepted as a matter of course in plenty of publications but earns a *New Maps* submission an automatic trip to the reject pile. But I believe magic—not the Harry Potter wand-waving kind, but magic as the word has been understood by mystics, occultists, healers, and mages for centuries, perhaps best summed up in Dion Fortune's oft-quoted definition, "the art and science of causing change in consciousness in accordance with will"—is a fairly incontrovertible part of the fabric of our reality. The placebo effect, for one example, could be considered a form of magic.

And so I formulated what's been my guideline for authors: "Stories may include elements of the metaphysical, supernatural, or paranormal, but only to the extent that you, the author, find it plausible that these things may actually happen in our world as you understand it."

But that story I received in March of 2021—which you can read at the end of this issue—made me think: What if we relaxed that requirement for just one issue, and let some really powerful magic in, some really pyrotechnic stuff? Keep it deindustrial, of course: powerful as it may be, it shouldn't find, or even seek to find, a way to perpetuate the fossil-fuel economy any longer than it would otherwise last. But what would a deindustrial world full of magic be like?

I proposed the possibility in an article in issue 1:2, and by issue 1:3 I'd heard positively from enough readers to greenlight it. Then I just waited for enough stories to come in. Over the months, occasional fantastic examples of this new flavor of magical realism—magic within a real world of ecological limits—found their way to me, and their authors patiently let me keep hold of them. Now, at the beginning of the third year of this magazine, here they finally are, and I hope you'll enjoy them as much as I have, and I've enjoyed them a lot.

—Nathanael Bonnell
Editor

Letters

New Maps *welcomes letters, whether to the editor or as part of a conversation between readers in the Letters section. Email* editor@new-maps.com, *with "Letter" somewhere in the subject line, and sign with your name as you'd like it to be printed. Or write via post, including your name and a note to consider your letter for publication, to Looseleaf Publishing, 87095 Valley Road, Bayfield, WI 54814, USA.*

Finding My Way to *New Maps*

In the letters section of the latest issue you asked what early political, philosophical or cultural leanings eventually made me find my way to new maps and deindustrial fiction.

For me, it was a combination of loving the land — and the animals on it like the wolves, bears, birds and other creatures plus design. Design might seem strange, but I run R&D and innovation programs. As I started looking into sustainability, and the needs for dramatic improvements in material and energy use, I realized that the only real leverage you had was design, Once you picked a solution, you were bound by the performance potential and systemic constraints of that solution.

A good example is choosing natural gas as a solution for climate change. It is still a carbon based fuel. You are unlikely to achieve net-zero burning carbon based fuels. At best, you are reducing the intensity of emissions, which is still a problem, especially if energy demand continues to grow.

From design, you start looking at systems and structures and realize that a lot of ideas that work at low volume, fail the scaling challenge. Think biofuels. Technically they can work. However, if you were to try to replace carbon based fuels for transportation around the world with renewable biofuels you would run out of land to grow food. It succeeds technically and fails systemically.

So, do the math. It's clear where the trajectory of our decision as a species is heading. As you recognize this, you start finding other people who see the same thing. I started with the Dark Mountain project who's manifesto acknowledges that "we live in a time of social, economic and ecological unravelling" and the need for new stories to learn how to live with it. And somehow, I found my way to New Maps. Great magazine by the way. I am enjoying it very much — thank you for bringing it to life. That is a real challenge in today's day and age and I commend you for your fortitude.

None of this makes me fatalistic or down on the world. Most of these forces are out of my control and wailing at them is a little like Don Quixote tilting at windmills. I have made my peace with that and simply do the best I can with what I have, with where I am and let the chips fall where they may. There's still a lot to be grateful for and to enjoy in life.

Shawn Gervais
Victoria, British Columbia

Shawn,

It seems like a big challenge to point to things that are technically feasible and explain to people that, despite the proof-of-concept that they can see in front of them, the idea is doomed because it's untenable in the broader context of the world. As you write, the foofaraw about a fusion reactor achieving $Q > 1$ a month or two ago is an obvious case in point. Okay, they ran 192 of the world's largest lasers and got out a little more energy than it took to run them. But if you cipher up the energy it took to create the exotic materials they needed for the experiment, for example the chamber capable of holding a reaction taking place at 100,000,000°C and the flood of neutrons coming off of it, the math looks a lot less promising. Even the fusion boosters are saying it's still a decade away, or maybe more, which is a tune we've been hearing long enough that they can play it on the oldies station.

You invoked the phrase "Do the math"—with your background, you may be interested in physics professor Tom Murphy's great blog by that name.[1] He explores a lot of the same kinds of thing you wrote about: whether the highly promoted green energy solutions can actually live up to their hype.

Thanks for the kind words about the magazine. I'm glad to be running it. Being analog-first in a digital world satisfies my willfully retrograde tendencies in a way I still enjoy after two years doing it. Making peace with the direction the world is headed is a challenge of its own; congratulations on making your peace with it. —NB

The idle railcars [See "Field Notes," previous issue. —Ed.] are sitting on the Wisconsin Great Northern tracks for several reasons. Many short line railroads have sections of track that are no longer in use. If they were in use the short line would not have them. Instead of tearing up the rails for scrap they utilize them by renting out space for railcar storage. Typical rental rates are $5 to $10 per day per railcar. Freight railcars cost 100K to 150K to build. They have a useful life of 50 years. It is in the self interest of the railcar owner to pay for storage instead of scrapping them for a few thousand dollars each. Past perverse federal tax policies have led to an overproduction of the national railcar fleet. In addition railroad companies have implemented a new management system called Precision Scheduled Railroading. This system speeds up the movement of railcars hence reducing the number of railcars needed. So to sum up the railcars are there because they are not needed at this time and the owners expect that they will become useful in the future.

Ross

Ross,

Thanks for the note, and the education on the railroads' economics. I didn't realize the railcar fleet had been overbuilt. I suppose in that way it's not unlike the railroad system itself, with the way that the original robber-barons who built it out were so focused on making money and so little interested in actually building a sensible rail system.[2]

It appears, then, that I missed my target in supposing that the idle railcars said something about economic contraction or

---

1 https://dothemath.ucsd.edu. Murphy has also contributed a piece in this issue.
2 Readers interested in this history will find it in Dee Brown's *Hear That Lonesome Whistle Blow* (New York, N.Y.: Henry Holt, 2001).

upheaval; it seems more correct to say that they simply represent a readjustment to economic equilibrium. Yet that in its way is its own indicator of the end of the age of excess. During the Industrial Revolution the U.S.'s infrastructure was built on its enormous abundance of resources, from timber to iron ore to petroleum, with the result that in the early 1900s, a town like Ashland, Wisconsin (then near its peak iron-boom population of 13,000), was at one point served by five different railroads. Of course the buildout of automobile roads was the biggest cause of the death of railroads, but another is the gradual reining in of that kind of prodigality, which was carried out substantially in service of bankers and investors. It's a subtler sign of the age of decline, perhaps, but also shows how long the storm has been gathering. —NB

LINGUISTICON

Dear Nathanael,

Your essay in the Fall 2023 issue, "Whither English?" got me all hyped up about the possibilities of language, linguistics, and wordplay in deindustrial fiction. You also referenced some great novels, and thinking of those got me rolling down a bowling lane of memories about some other striking reads I've read. Two that immediately sprang to mind were Russell Hoban's *Riddley Walker*, and Samuel R. Delany's *Babel-17*.

I first read Hoban's book when I was deep into my obsession with David Tibet and his "apocalyptic folk" music project, Current 93. The book had been one of the inspirations behind the album *Of Ruine or Some Blazing Starre*, and that album being one of my favorites of theirs, I followed the track of influence backwards to find out what had roused Tibet's lyrical imagination. I have never been disappointed in reading or listening to the things that had obsessed Tibet, and the case with the book by Hoban was no different. Hint's of Hoban's influence are scattered around on several other Current 93 albums as well.

It wasn't until I looked up Hoban at the library that I realized I already had a connection to the author. My mom and grandma had loved to read me his children's book *The Little Brute Family*, and I loved to hear them read it. His other children's book *Frances the Badger* is more well-known and won him lasting acclaim, and he became prolific in the realm of children's literature. His many adult novels sit across a spectrum of genres from biting literary realism to science fiction and fantasy, and have often been described as magic-realist. *Riddley Walker* sits comfortably in the subgenre of post-apocalyptic SF, and is also a literary and linguistic masterpiece.

The language is what makes the work so unique. It's written in a kind of retro-future patois based on the English dialect as spoken in Kent, where the novel is set some years hence after nuclear war has ravaged the world. The book is presented as a document written by the main character, and the words of this pidgin are spelled out phonetically, adding to the richness of the created world, and challenging the reader to really get into the headspace of the character.

The time period around when I read *Riddley Walker* was also when I happened to be deep into my parallel obsession with the work of Samuel R. Delany. *Dhalgren* had shattered my mind (in a good way) and inspired me to be more serious in my own desire to write. I devoured most of his other books shortly thereafter. *Babel-17* remains one of the standouts from his copious output.

The power of language to shape awareness, along lines suggested by the Sapir–Whorf hypothesis, is one of the book's main themes. This hypothesis proposes that the language a person speaks directly influences the way that person thinks about reality. Rydra Wong is the main character in this novel, and she is a poet, translator, and space captain fluent in myriad languages, including a variety of sign languages. She is given a mission to interpret the mysterious alien code known as Babel-17 and track down where it is coming from. In the course of her investigation she learns it is not a military or communication code, but a language. As she begins the process of learning the language she comes to understand it has no concept of "you" or "I"—and that it can cause radical changes in the consciousness and behavior of the people who use it, making them slip into psychosis and act out as sociopaths.

(If there is truth in the Sapir–Whorf hypotheis it makes me wonder what net effect corporate-business-managerese has on the world?)

I'm sure there are many other speculative fiction novels that I haven't gotten around to reading yet where the elements and ideas surrounding language are dialed up, and I'd love to hear from any *New Maps* readers who have suggestions. What works do you like that have twisted up the tongues? Reading all of this kind of material is a very healthy way to learn how we can amp up our own linguistic conjectures within the deindustrial genre.

Sincerely,
Justin Patrick Moore

Justin,
You're not the first person to recommend Riddley Walker *to me, and it seems clear that I'll soon need to find a copy, and possibly review the book here. All these recommendations sound quite interesting, and your mention of Current 93's work (which I haven't yet listened to) reminds me that I've considered before publishing reviews of deindustrial music. Another reader previously proposed a review of the Boards of Canada's* Tomorrow's Harvest *(it has yet to materialize), and I've thought myself about mentioning the band Bowerbirds, particularly on the merit of their song "The Marbled Godwit," along with perhaps Muse's* The 2nd Law *and in particular the song "Unsustainable." I'd appreciate any other readers' recommendations on music. Meanwhile, the books you mentioned go onto the growing to-read pile!*
—NB

ESSAYS & SUNDRIES

Legend Tripping, the Deindustrial Gothic, and a World Full of Monsters

Monsters exist because they are part of the divine plan, and in the horrible features of those same monsters the power of the Creator is revealed.
—Umberto Eco, *The Name of the Rose*

Cheap Thrills
Speculations on Entertainment, Media, Art, and Leisure in the Deindustrial Age
Justin Patrick Moore

In our so-called rationalist and reasonable age, legends have lost none of their currency and have persisted and flourished in new guises well into industrial times. Our modern urban legends show this, and like older legends they are also often associated with very specific places. The activity of legend-tripping to these places has grown up around and alongside these twice-told tales, and seems to have really taken off since the 1950s. The pastime of legend-tripping takes a person on a thrill ride through the spine-tingling borderlands where folklore mingles with historical facts, where rites of passage expose one to ethereal dangers, and into those Gothic places where ghosts and monsters are said to have made their homes. The legend trip leads people past the familiar and on a magical journey into the unknown.

The chances are strong that if you grew up in America, or some other industrialized nation, you've already been on a legend trip. If you've ever snuck into a cemetery at night to visit a particular grave associated with ghosts, hauntings, or alleged crimes, you've legend-tripped. If you've ever driven to a particular bridge or to a specific bend in the road, where you then have to turn off the car and flash the headlights three times to see if you can hear the screams of the children who were said to have died in a school bus wreck at that very spot, you've legend-tripped. If you have ever snuck into an abandoned building, or a building you *thought* was abandoned, because a witch was said to have lived there, or a serial killer was said to have taken his victims there, you have dosed yourself up on a legend. If you ever tried to find the place where the Frogman climbed out of the Little Miami River and over the guardrail to amble in front of passing traffic, with the hope that you might see a Frogman as well, then you have legend-tripped.

In all of these examples the story came first, often in the form of an urban legend, but how did these stories start and where did they come from? Although some academic folklorists prefer to call them *contemporary legends* the name *urban legends* is still what actual folk prefer to refer to them as. Author and professor Jan Harold Brunvand brought the term urban legend into general use for the public in his 1981 book *The Vanishing Hitchhiker: American Urban Legends and Their Meaning*. Though the stories that become urban legends are popular enough on their own, Brunvand's book and his subsequent follow-ups helped popularize many stories even further, where they continued to take on new life.

Urban legends are born of rumor, misremembered history, unexplained experiences, and can't-explain experiences. The urban legend is at home when something from beyond is seen, felt or heard, then whispered about and spread on playgrounds and bus rides, told at a party, and passed on from one person to another.

At its most basic, a legend trip can be defined as an excursion to a place where something uncanny has happened. These legend trips are undertaken for the most part by adolescents, often under the influence of alcohol, marijuana or other drugs.[1] Often the people who go on the trip have the specific intention of having an uncanny experience of their own. In part it may be to test the veracity of the legend. In part it may be to test their strength, willpower, and courage. In this latter mode the legend trip also takes on aspects of a rite of passage. Rites of passage and rituals in general are often noted for their liminality. Visiting places associated with threshold experiences acts as a way of accessing the altered space, often in an altered state, and functions as a way of passing through, of passing a test.

Brunvand wrote in his *Encyclopedia of Urban Legends* that "Legend trips function both as informal tests of the claims made in supernatural legends and as verification of the courage of the teens themselves, who may try to act out the legends they have heard by blinking the car lights a certain number of times, calling out for the ghost, or sitting on a cursed gravestone."

Much of the time these trips happen at night, as the darkness adds to the spook factor, though it's hardly a requirement with anything as informal as a legend trip. The places themselves are usually alleged to be the scene of tragedy or salacious crime, or a haunting, monster sighting, or other form of paranormal activity. Bill Ellis wrote in the *American Folklore Encyclopedia* that "often a baby is said to have died or been murdered, frequently at a bridge, and its ghost is said to cry at certain times. Or a person—man or woman—was decapitated in an accident, and a ghostly light lingers at the site of the tragedy."

---

1 With the use of hallucinogens it becomes a real head trip. I'm not necessarily recommending this.

The legend trip is a distinctly North American phenomenon, though it is not necessarily unknown outside this continent. For some it isn't just a teenage rite of passage either, but something that becomes a way life, an all-consuming activity that draws them to site after site, story after story throughout adulthood. I think this is in part because of the ever-present human hunger for stories, and the trips don't exist without the legends. For repeat offenders who go on to visit site after site, it becomes a way of collecting stories, and involving themselves in the story. I think the popularity of this activity also has to do with a thirst for magic and mystery. For those who have gone from mere enthusiast to true cult fanatic, the documentation of their own experiences in the form of podcasts, vlogs, articles, and books becomes a part of the game. In time they may go on to become bona fide true-crime, paranormal, and occult investigators.

Urban Exploration and the Deindustrial Gothic

Going on legend trips routinely crosses over into the activity of urban exploration and the practice of psychogeography. Setting is character, and the often horrific and bloody stories associated with many sites might be seen as a reflection of the wretched state of our collective inner lives in the shared outer landscape. The inner aspect the location, first known through the stories, then touches the outer life when these places are visited. New experiences, in turn, get reflected upon and internalized, and when shared with others, send further refractions of the tale out into the culture.

Though locations vary from region to region certain categories of places remain common: bridges, tunnels, caves, cemeteries, abandoned buildings, a particular grove of trees in the woods, or a certain stretch of lonely road. For the most part they are places that have been left untended and abandoned. An empty house is commensurate with the experience of urban and rural decay and it is easy to imagine how they might be haunted. Our collective psyche provides ample material for stories about haunted houses as most everyone has heard heart-wrenching tales of dysfunctional families, of wife beaters and child abusers. Those who live in this unfortunate reality abide in everyday haunted houses. Sometimes they leave behind ghosts and psychic traumas that echo in our shared memory.

I think it is worth noting that in Gothic literature the action of a story always seem to unfold in places that are decaying and falling apart. The settings are often moldering estates and castles, decrepit houses and abandoned ruins, a similarity shared with some deindustrial tales set in the time of decline and future dark ages. Gloom and desolation hang over everything. The settings are also relatively isolated from outside help. In this respect, Detroit could be one of the most

Gothic, and deindustrial, cities in North America. Many other once prosperous towns and cities across the United States and around the world could now be considered paramours of a deindustrial Gothic sensibility. They become subject to photographers and artists making ruin porn, documenting the slow demise of buildings as nature, the elements and humans enact their destruction. Visiting these places is another kind of legend trip.

As Jhonn Balance of the band Coil sang, "Pay your respects to the vultures / for they are your future."[2] The popularity of ruin porn and urban exploration of abandoned sites lies in the fact that it is an exposure to the unavoidable death of our own mortal coils. As our own civilization succumbs to the natural cycle of growth and decline, ruin porn reminds us of the processes to which we will all succumb.

Abandoned amusement parks are particularly popular for those touring the ruins of deindustrial civilization. Perhaps it is because they can be seen as representing a kind of peak experience in industrial culture: the rides, attractions, sights, sounds, and tastes all reinforce the spectacle of getting what you want when you want it, if you can afford the price of the ticket. Seeing nature take over places where the good times once rolled down coaster tracks is perhaps a reminder that the days of frivolous consumption are not as eternal as many media messages have implied.

In a society that obsessed with ideas of limitless progress, the allure of ruin porn and the exploration of industrial ruins is an escape valve offering a look at inevitable endings. The fallacy of perpetual economic growth gets stripped down and laid bare. All things eventually sink into the underworld before they can be reborn.

Into the Underworld

Since ancient times, certain spots were thought of as being entrances to the underworld, and mythic figures such as Aeneas and Hercules passed through those gates in the course of their adventures. For Aeneas and Hercules the portal happened to be a cave near Lake Avernus, whose waters were gathered in a volcanic crater. When the hero Odysseus visited the underworld, he went by way of the River Acheron in northwest Greece. In our own time numerous stories about places named as the "Gates of Hell" or "Pits of Hell" persist within the milieu of urban legends. There are numerous places around the United States alone rumored to be portals to the underworld.

The Pits of Hell in Columbus, Ohio, is one such spot. It is a large underground tunnel and drainage culvert in Clintonville Park (at the time of this writ-

---

2 Coil, "The Last Amethyst Deceiver," from *The Ape of Naples*.

ing renamed "Portal Park" by users on Google Maps). The Pit can be accessed with convenience from behind the parking lot of a Tim Horton's coffeeshop. The place is also known as the Gates of Hell and the Blood Bowl. It is a massive industrial presence with huge steel I-beams at the mouth of a basin, at the bottom of which is a large drainage tunnel, all of it covered in tags and graffiti. The name Blood Bowl came to the place, according to the stories, when a local skateboarder died trying to do a stunt in the tunnel. When he failed to land his trick he hit his head hard on the concrete and his blood was spattered everywhere. In the center of the tunnel is a chamber where it is said the more impressive pieces of graffiti art can be found. I can imagine this chamber being a popular place to get high and drink beer or cough syrup for teenagers (if teenagers are still "allowed" to sneak away from their helicopter parents long enough to do these things).

In the town of York, Pennsylvania, is a place where there are not just one, but Seven Gates of Hell. Located on Trout Run Road, formerly named Toad Road, the place is associated with that modern form of barbarism known to many as psychiatry. It is said that a lunatic asylum was once located off this road in the 1800s. When it caught fire, many of the inmates burned to death in the devouring flames, as firefighters couldn't reach it in time. Hundreds of others used the fire as their chance to escape into the woods. Search parties were sent to collect these poor souls, who only wanted their freedom. The searchers were aggressive when they apprehended the escapees. Their heads had been filled by many stories of the violent and crazed behavior of the people locked away inside. The searchers were said to have beaten many of the escapees into submission, and those who wouldn't submit they murdered. As if the torture of these "patients" inside the asylum walls by dubious therapeutic techniques hadn't been enough, their subsequent deaths by fire and violence are said to have left a psychic stain on the land that led to the opening of these Seven Gates of Hell.

The land home to the Seven Gates gives would-be legend-trippers a bit of trouble because they are located on private property. For teenagers the act of trespassing most likely adds to the thrill, but for adults who would prefer to keep their trips on the legal side of the law, this kind of escapades might best be avoided.

Those of drinking age might be better off visiting another Gate to Hell that is said to exist in the basement of Bobby Mackey's Music World, a country-music night club in Wilder, Kentucky. It sits at 44 Licking Pike, just above the banks of the north-flowing Licking River, one of the tributaries to the Ohio River. The story has it that there was a slaughterhouse on the site in the 19th century. It got torn down and a roadhouse was built on the spot that went under various names until country singer and musician Bobby Mackey bought the joint. While having a portal to Hell in the basement might have been enough to put Mackey's club on the map, no self-respecting night club owner should let a good haunting go to waste: his venue is also alleged to be the abode of the ghost of Pearl Bryan, an Indiana woman who was brutally murdered and decapitated in 1896 a few miles away in Fort Thomas, Kentucky.

The story of Pearl Bryan is one of many gruesome chapters in Greater Cincinnati's book of true crime. Bryan was a socialite from Greencastle, Indiana. Her father was a well respected and wealthy dairy farmer, and she was well liked and regarded as beautiful throughout the community. Scott Jackson was an aspiring dentist who happened to pass through her hometown, and the two had a love affair. When Jackson left for dental school in Cincinnati he also left her knocked up with a child. She had just started working as a Sunday school teacher when this happened, and she decided to track Jackson down. Without wanting to cause a scandal, she told her parents she was going to visit a friend in Indianapolis, but instead went to Cincinnati to look for the man who jilted her and tell him she was pregnant, hopeful that they would marry. Instead he and an accomplice Alonzo M. Walling dosed her up with cocaine, took her to a secluded spot just across the river in Kentucky, and decapitated her while she was still alive on January 31, 1896. Her headless body was found shortly thereafter by a farmhand. Jackson and Walling were later apprehended, and sentenced for murder, for which they were hanged the following year behind the Campbell County Courthouse. The first drop of the rope was not enough to snap their wicked necks, and it took them a few minutes to strangle to death on the gallows. These two criminals have the odd distinction of being the last to die by the noose in Campbell County.

Some friends of mine once went on a trip to visit a few sites in Indiana. Their trip wasn't so much about chasing legends as it was a form of legend-tripping's sister or cousin, so called "dark tourism," or travel to places associated with death and suffering. Their first stops were the blink-and-you-miss-them towns of Linn and Crete, Indiana, two burgs associated with the birth and life of notorious cult leader Jim Jones. Then on the next leg of their jaunt, they visited the town of Greencastle. There they visited the cemetery and unmarked gravestone of Pearl Bryan, who was buried without her head, the location of which was never revealed by her murderers. Bryan's gravestone has been left unmarked because it kept on getting stolen by people who would make dark pilgrimages to the place.

I Want to Believe in Monsters

Monsters such as the murderers Jackson and Walling aren't the only ones to haunt our memories or cause people to trip out on a legend. Sites associated with monsters such as the Loveland Frog Man, the Pope Lick Monster, the Lake

Erie Monster, Bigfoot, and the Mothman have become places of veneration and pilgrimage for those who hope to see one of these beings themselves. While the existence of these beings is denied by official science, it is embraced by those with a sense of the mythic.

One town that has become a major destination spot for monster lovers is Point Pleasant, West Virginia. It holds an annual Mothman festival every third weekend in September to commemorate the original sightings of the red-eyed and winged being in 1966. The festival draws a huge crowd every year and has become an important part of the town's economic survival. Seekers who are also interested in the nearby mysteries of the Flatwoods monster often attend. I can see a situation arising in our deindustrial futures where local festivals and holidays emerge around other monstrous creatures, with celebrations happening on dates associated with their first sightings or major dates of their monstrous activity. As the festivals transform over time, they might begin to include offerings and rituals as ways of appeasing the wrath of the monsters, and of keeping their community prosperous and protected.

Cryptids are another term people use for these kinds of beings, and in the past I used that word interchangeably for monster without really thinking about nuances of definition. As I reread sections of John Michael Greer's book *Monsters: An Investigator's Guide to Magical Beings* for this article, I noticed he deliberately does not used the word cryptid. Greer gave the explanation that a cryptid can be any kind of unknown creature. It could be an undiscovered kind of sardine or a newfangled rat, or an unknown microfauna deep within the sea. In this sense cryptids are simply classes of creatures that humans haven't encountered before. Monsters, on the other hand, have been encountered by many people, and they become part of the folklore of their region and have stories and lore surrounding them. They may be real physical creatures *and* they may exist solely on levels of non-material reality such as the astral plane. Some monsters exist on multiple levels of reality and consciousness. What distinguishes them from the cryptid is the accretion of stories surrounding them and their encounters with humans. All that said, many popular blogs, YouTube channels, and books that delve into these subjects don't often make this distinction and call these kinds of beings cryptids.

A genuine need for monster seekers might arise as our societies slip from their current stages deeper into the deindustrial Gothic landscapes. Within the ruins of aged estates, crumbling mental asylums, and tweaked-out hospitals, not all the ghosts that linger will be mere abstractions, and intrepid questers with the skills to cope with these beings and ameliorate their influence in communities will be needed. The skills such investigators need are not currently taught in the university—another place where the wrecked shells of buildings may leave behind vicious postmodern imprints on the *genius loci*.

Becoming a monster investigator in your spare time, however, is certainly feasible, and another activity that doesn't require much in terms of equipment or expensive gear. Maps of your local area and some books on local folklore are enough to get you started, along with notebooks to write down and sketch observations and findings. A camera and tape recorder could be added to the kit, used to interview witnesses and people knowledgeable of local lore and to document sightings. Greer's book *Monsters* is one of the best places to start, with a whole chapter devoted to the art of investigation. The information in Greer's book, when combined with that in the guidebook for urban exploration by Ninjalicious, *Access All Areas*, can lay a groundwork of two different skill sets required for navigating the inner and outer landscapes where monsters dwell.

Chances are, no matter where you live, there is a storied place nearby for you to visit. Some of these are perhaps already destination spots for legend-trippers. Others might be trip sites that are waiting to be born. A great resource for North Americans is *The Map in Black: A Mysterious Map of North America*,[3] created by Jeff Craig. *The Map in Black* shows sites categorized under Aliens, UFOs, Ancient American Sites, Cryptids (that usage of the word again!), Ecology, Hauntings, Military/Government sites, Native Lands, and Sacred Geography. These are all perfect categories to look at when planning a legend trip. At the time of this writing the internet is still intact and there are numerous websites devoted to the hobbies of urban exploration, legend-tripping, and visiting mysterious places. When the internet is gone books on local folklore, ghost stories, and urban legends will be the places to check for ideas. The next legend-tripping site will be born when someone follows up on a rumor another person told them while out skateboarding together, or in the office, and they go to check the place out for themselves, and then tell others about the spot in turn.

Legend trips are all about the stories we tell ourselves. By visiting these places we have the chance of embodying the stories, of touching a place where something mysterious happened. In so doing we can allow their magic and mystery to come into our lives.

Re/sources

Belanger, Jeff. *Picture Yourself Legend Tripping: Your Complete Guide to Finding UFOs, Monsters, Ghosts, and Urban Legends in Your Own Backyard*. Boston, Mass.: Cengage Learning PTR, 2010.

Brunvand, Jan Harold. *The Vanishing Hitchhiker: American Urban Legends and Their Meaning*. New York, N.Y.: Norton, 1981.

Brunvand, Jan Harold, ed. *American Folklore: An Encyclopedia*. New York, N.Y.: Garland Publishing Inc., 1996.

---

3   www.mapinblack.com

Greer, John Michael. *Monsters: An Investigator's Guide to Magical Beings.* Lewes, England: Aeon Publishing, 2021.

Hensley, Douglas. *Hell's Gate: Terror at Bobby Mackey's Music World (America's Most Documented Haunting).* Denver, Colo.: Outskirts Publishing, 2005.

Kownacki, Paul. "Columbus, Ohio—Pit of Hell." RoadsideAmerica.com, Mar. 12, 2009. https://www.roadsideamerica.com/tip/20632

Lyons, Siobhan. "What 'Ruin Porn' Tells Us About Ruins—And Porn." CNN Style, Nov. 1, 2017. https://www.cnn.com/style/article/what-ruin-porn-tells-us-about-ruins-and-porn/index.html

Malvern Jr., Marcus. "The Downingtown Gates of Hell." Weird U.S., n.d. http://www.weirdus.com/states/pennsylvania/local_legends/seven_gates_of_hell/

Wikipedia contributors. "Gates of Hell." *Wikipedia.* https://en.wikipedia.org/wiki/Gates_of_hell (accessed Jan. 2023).

Book Reviews

Carrie Vaughn's Coast Road World

We have been writing books about imaginary apocalypses for a long, long time, apparently since the 13th century (according to Wikipedia.)[1] Indeed I have read many of them, from *On the Beach* by Nevil Shute (nuclear war — no survivors) by way of *Alas, Babylon* by Pat Frank (nuclear war — rather nice little enclave survives comfortably) to more nuanced apocalypses like *The Girl with All the Gifts* by M. R. Carey, *The Road* by Cormac McCarthy, and a great many more. The causes of apocalypses have become numerous and varied. What started as mainly nuclear holocaust extended to include climate catastrophes, famine, plague, electromagnetic pulses and solar flares, and even zombies. I have read a fair number of these and have quite enjoyed a few of them.

Bannerless and **The Wild Dead** by Carrie Vaughn
Harper Voyager, 2017 and 2018
Review by Yvonne Rowse

Far more interesting to me have been the post-apocalypse books: for example *Dies the Fire* by S. M. Stirling, *Station Eleven* by Emily St. John Mandel, and *Earth Abides* by George Stewart. To be fair, most apocalypse books segue into what happens afterwards and mostly what happens afterwards is deindustrial fiction.

The two Coast Road novels are set in a post-apocalyptic world. They are detective novels whose focus is only peripherally the apocalypse and the subsequent recovery.

Both novels are murder investigations. The point of view character, Enid, is a young investigator who travels with her partner to the scene of the death. It is

---

1 "List of apocalyptic and post-apocalyptic fiction." Accessed January 2023.

her job to investigate the crime, find out who committed it and make an initial judgment about how to deal with the perpetrator.

As noted, both novels are murder investigations. Murder and theft are crimes that are pretty much the same in any society but there are other crimes that are particular to a society. For example, atheism is a capital crime in some countries, and at one time the making, selling and consuming of alcohol was a crime in the U.S. In the Coast Road communities, in addition to the traditional crimes, it is illegal to have a baby without permission and to exceed the quotas set for harvesting food. To understand the crimes and the motivations for the crimes, one must have some understanding of the society.

The novels are set maybe seventy years after The Fall, a set of connected disasters that led to an almost complete societal breakdown. Vaughn herself writes:

> Climate change brings mega storms and rising sea levels, compounded with failing infrastructure because of bad policy, compounded with a Great Depression or worse level economic crash, and compound *that* with a 1918 Spanish flu level epidemic. The kind of apocalypse I imagined required literally *everything* going wrong. It seemed a little farfetched when I started.[2]

She published the first book, *Bannerless*, in 2017. Since then we have had droughts, floods, wildfires, infrastructure issues, and a Covid pandemic, together with resource depletion resulting in inflation and increasing polarization and violence within the population. None of these have lead to The Fall yet but one could imagine that the accelerating problems are definitely heading in that direction.

The society the writer envisages emerging in one small area of the west coast of America is quite fascinating. Devastating storms have not gone away; the world hasn't returned to "normal" after The Fall. Harvest failure and hunger are an ever-present threat and as a consequence the society is tightly controlled. Quotas are set for the amount of resources that can be exploited and these are rigidly enforced. Failure to reach quota will mean hunger and a less comfortable life; exceeding quota is a potentially a crime because it will result in impoverishment for the people of the future.

Many technologies were lost during The Fall but this small area of the country retained medical knowledge and managed to develop an effective birth control implant as well as antiseptics and antibiotics. Based on these technologies a

---

2 Vaughn, Carrie. "Five Things I Learned While Writing *The Wild Dead*." Terribleminds (blog), Aug. 1, 2018. http://terribleminds.com/ramble/2018/08/01/carrie-vaughn-five-things-i-learned-writing-the-wild-dead/

system has developed where the town committee will grant a household a Banner, an indication that the household has worked hard and is meeting its quota so that a baby can be supported and raised to adulthood. This skews the society in very interesting ways. Every child is wanted and treasured; however, given the restrictions, there is an obsession with achieving a banner. The darker side to this is that people connive to cheat on quotas, the households of women who have a bannerless baby are broken up, and those people born bannerless often suffer lifelong stigma.

The first novel, *Bannerless*, sees Enid investigating a death in Pasadan. The man who has died is suspected by the village of being bannerless and as a consequence is very much an outsider in this otherwise idyllic-seeming village. Unlike in a modern investigation there is no forensic science. The victim has usually been dead for a number of days because there is no very quick method of getting from place to place and no refrigeration. A lot of the investigation is old-fashioned questioning and piecing information and motives together. Enid and her partner spend a lot of time walking between households trying to get a clear view of what happened.

In between each chapter concerning the investigation there is a chapter about Enid's earlier life. This slows the story down somewhat but gives an increased level of insight into how the wider community works. We see different types of settlements still living under the same rules, and come to understand the importance of messengers and wandering minstrels. There are way stations on the road for those caught out by storms or needing a place to stay on their travels.

We also meet the "wild" people who live in the ruins to the east of the Coast Road. The wild people are living even closer to the edge of starvation, mostly foraging and hunting and making use of the abundance of salvage available in the ruins. They could join the Coast Road community but fear their children being taken from them and the loss of freedom and autonomy that they perceive, rightly, would be required.

It is during the investigation sections that we get a clear understanding of the powers of the investigators. After one of the committee members disputes their authority Enid says,

> You're right. If you don't want us here, we don't have to stay. We only have the authority you let us have. But if we leave, if you reject us, you give up the right to trade with any other town on the Coast Road. Anything you need supplied by anyone else? Gone. None of you will ever be allowed to settle anywhere else. No one else will have you. Outcast from the whole of civilization. Is that what you want?

The investigation is concluded satisfactorily with the traditional reveal to all parties and a suitable judgment. The real punishment is that everyone up and down the Coast Road would know of the events and who was to blame and, in a society built on cooperation, this would be hard.

The second novel, *The Wild Dead*, starts with Enid, accompanied by a new young and inexperienced partner, traveling to The Estuary to mediate a simple dispute about whether the wider community should be required to help shore up a pre-Fall building, now in a parlous and dangerous state. Whilst the investigators view the building a body is found, a young woman on the sands with her throat cut. Thus begins an unexpected murder investigation.

This is a much more straightforward book than the first one as most of the worldbuilding has already been done. The victim turns out to be from one of the outsider camps, one of the wild folk.

The Coast Road community we meet here is just a little short of dysfunctional. There had been a woman who cut out her implant some twenty years earlier, resulting in the breakup of her previous household, and there is still a great deal of bitterness between the community and the new household, Last House, that has taken in the woman.

Against this background Enid tries to establish the identity of the victim and who murdered her. Her new partner, Teeg, is very keen not to address this murder and, when Enid insists, wants to pin the murder on one of the inhabitants of Last House. Enid journeys into the wild to attempt to find the truth from the victim's family. Teeg refuses to go and when Enid returns with illuminating information, Teeg has already headed back with his suspect to report Enid lost, possibly dead.

Even though this book was a reread it kept me awake into the night until I had finished it. I cared about the characters and wanted to see the right person brought to justice.

I have seen these books described as dystopian and they may well look that way. Personal liberty is restricted for the good of society and we don't see the details of how all of this is controlled and balanced. As mentioned above, the most severe punishment appears to be shunning. A person, household or village that is shunned by the rest of this society will be terribly isolated and, given that the small scale of each settlement requires some level of trading to survive, face a gradual or fast decline. It is not a merciful punishment. Those breaking the social contract would definitely regard this as a dystopia. On the other hand, in a world where survival is dependent on cooperation, for those abiding by the rules it could look pretty utopian.

Linked to these two books are two short stories. "Where Would You Be

Now"[3] tells of the end of The Fall and the beginning of this new society. "Amaryllis"[4] is set on a fishing boat captained by a bannerless woman and demonstrates how difficult it is to be born bannerless, and the unfair stigma attached to it. Both are interesting short stories, available on the web, and well worth reading.

This world was written by a woman who is a New York Times bestselling author mainly, I think, for her urban fantasy books. This, however, is straight deindustrial fiction and I love it. I wish she would write more in the Coast Road world.

A Kid for a New World

Michael Perry is a local celebrity up here in northern Wisconsin. His fame is due mostly to hosting shows at the Big Top Chautauqua down the road from *New Maps* HQ, which get syndicated on Wisconsin Public Radio, and to writing folksy books like *Population: 485: Meeting Your Neighbors One Siren at a Time* and *Truck: A Love Story*. So it was something of a surprise to me to discover, by chance, that he's written a deindustrial sci-fi novel for young adults.

The Scavengers
Michael Perry
HarperCollins, 2014
Review: Nathanael Bonnell

Surprise (and my age difference from the target audience) notwithstanding, I quickly found myself drawn in. The book's mixture of poignant and funny is evident from the very beginning when we're introduced to the protagonist, a girl of about 10 or 12 who lives on an abandoned junkyard with her family and a vicious rooster with a hacking cough. It's clear that her family is desperately hard-put, and equally clear that her relationship with them is strained. But she takes this mostly in stride and deals with it by moving out of their shack and down the hill into a mostly intact car from which she also takes a new name:

> I climbed up on the hood and stood there with my steel-toed boots planted wide and I wedged my fists on my hips and I announced that Maggie was yesterday, and from this day forward I would answer only to Ford Falcon. Ford, because we had a lot of rivers to cross. Falcon, because, well, if you have a lot of rivers to cross, a pair of wings can't hurt …

3   Tor, 2018. https://www.tor.com/2018/02/07/where-would-you-be-now-carrie-vaughn/
4   *Lightspeed*, 2010. http://www.lightspeedmagazine.com/fiction/amaryllis/

("Yes," she quickly admits, "I know. I named myself after an old dead car. Worse yet, it's not even a cool car. It's a station wagon.")

In Ford Falcon's world, the post-fossil-fuel future has arrived, but it's certainly not evenly distributed. A few years back most of the country's cities were put under Bubbles, and everyone had to choose for themselves whether to live under them—closely controlled—or OutBubble, where law and order are administered by whatever weapons you can find or make. OutBubble, oxen have replaced trucks, electricity is a fading memory, and the last vestige of culture left to Ford's family is an Emily Dickinson book they left the city with. It might be a paradise for small farmers except that nearly all arable land is property of the Bubble Cities and fenced off with the kind of voltage that would stop a T. rex.

Ford has distant memories of living with modern amenities before her family left, but doesn't feel much attachment to them. In her family's precarious situation she's forged an identity for a new world, as a kid who carries a club spiked with hog tusks and doesn't take nonsense from anyone, but still likes to snuggle up with her mom to read Emily with some brewed herbs. She's aided and abetted by her neighbor and mentor Toad, a 78-year-old man who speaks in spoonerisms and gives her a copy of *The American Boy's Handy Book* to keep her supplied with projects and trouble.

This uneasy equilibrium is destroyed one day when Ford comes home to find her parents' house raided and no one there. Once she's found her little brother Dookie—who's never learned to speak in coherent words but hasn't let that stop him from becoming a mischievous pest—she, Toad, and Toad's tough and homey wife Arlinda regroup and work on figuring out how to find her family again. Clues are scarce, but they have friends, know-how, and tenacity, and none of them lets anything keep them down for long.

The Scavengers shares several aspects with the last young-adult novels I reviewed here, Paolo Bacigalupi's *Ship Breaker* duology: a world sharply divided into haves and have-nots, a background of feuding warlord-level powers, and even genetically modified predators who've escaped from their lab to maraud around the edges of the plot (here, "solar bears," a well-meaning attempt to keep polar bears around in some form after the Arctic ice melted). But where Bacigalupi's protagonists were constantly fearful, Ford bounces back from anything with more determination than before, and where Bacigalupi's world was grim with occasional somewhat cheerful moments, Perry's world is one where people are finding their way in a new world, occasionally fumbling with the stress of it but largely adapting okay. The hope in the *Ship Breaker* books is exceedingly dim, but in this book it lights the way.

The love for rural life that underpins Michael Perry's other books is present everywhere in this one too. Ford, Toad, and Arlinda are all people deeply *of* their land, beset as it may be by outside interests, and they revel in the freedom of living OutBubble and knowing how to make up their own rules. The forces arrayed against them, it becomes clear, have little connection to the land, and that will make all the difference in their ability to figure out something to do about it.

Besides its rural dimension, though, and perhaps even more affectingly, this book is a tribute and a gift to the next generation. Perry dedicates it to his daughters and it's clear that he has been watching the way things are going and wondering with some unease about what kind of world they will live in. Ford, though, is unabashedly and unflinchingly a girl of her time. While her parents long for the creature comforts of a past they can't return to, Ford is adventurous, tough, and up for anything. Kids like her are the ones who'll slowly build a new order in a world that's freshly overturned and still in flux. And the future will be lucky to have them.

Two Haiku

Tom Murphy

I'm no poet, preferring prose for its clarity and completeness. So please forgive this amateur attempt to capture two opposing views on planetary limits in haiku form. One gracefully respects constraints, while the other … well, you'll see.

> *Just as in haiku*
> *Earth imposes hard limits*
> *We must live within*

And in the red corner:

> *It's preposterous*
> *To think that human imagination is lim …*

Buzzer. Disqualified. Nice try. And the winner is …

STORIES

Justin Patrick Moore

A Rat in the Cell

Chad left the offices of Zexol Galaxcient Imaging in a hurry, headed straight for the stairs into the subway, passed his pinky-finger smart ring over the sensor of the turnstile, dashed through the security scans. On the platform it smelled of equal parts train brake dust and the antiseptic aerosol disinfectants sprayed by the misters from the ceiling every fifteen minutes. To his annoyance, a busker dressed in a ratty and tattered fur coat played a squeezebox to the delight of a married couple and their two children.

Tourists, Chad snorted under his breath. He thought of telling the guards just to be a prick. Busking on the platform was illegal after all.

As the station filled up, a girl with shoulder-length sandy-blonde hair and a jean jacket sporting some band buttons brushed up against him, a paper cup of coffee clutched in her right hand, and her phone in the other.

"Sorry 'bout that," she muttered. She looked away to the digital train schedule on the board, a flustered look on her face, hoping she wouldn't be late for her new job as evening errand girl for one of the power couples who lived in a fancy gated community just outside the city.

In the bright fluorescent light of the station he saw the freckles around her ears with clarity, her chipped and bitten fingernails, and he could smell her sweat underneath a light floral perfume. Chad licked his lips. He was getting hungry.

When the train arrived he held back for just a moment, then followed her on and sat down next to her, just one seat away. It was Thursday night and he had Friday off, a three-day weekend sprawled out before him. There was a lot of work he wanted to catch up on, many toys he was eager to extrude from his 3D printer, spreads to look at from last weekend's private photo shoot of the hired model that he wanted to look at before he uploaded them to his website. He pulled out his phone and started flicking through the pictures, dragging and dropping the ones he liked into a folder.

The train was still boarding and to his annoyance when he looked up, the family had come on and sat across from him. It irritated him even further when the musician boarded and took up a spot in the corner of the car. A thin gray-haired Asian man sat across from the musician clutching a bag of produce between his feet. A black teenager wearing a green hoodie and with a silver backpack and skateboard scooted on with a few other stragglers. The doors shut and they started to move.

He had a long ride ahead of him, all the way to the end of the line. His condo was in one of the gated communities just outside the city. He'd been able to score a pad there just after he'd gotten his promotion to one of the project manager positions at Zexol. He had started off at the advertisng firm in graphic design. His climb up to the top had been a ruthless, cutthroat operation as he stepped on the backs of his fellow coworkers , but he'd succeeded in the end and could now afford a life among the posh.

He opened up the Securvulent app on his phone which fed him still shots and live streams from the security cameras he'd placed around his home. Seeing that everything was just so and in its place, he tapped another button on the phone for the Spyaven program, entered an eight-digit number. The screen dissolved into a new display that showed the hacked social media feeds of some of the women he stalked online. Then he checked his feeds from the stalker drone service he subscribed to using cryptocurrency on the some of the seediest sites the dark web had to offer.

He zoomed through these feeds, disappointed there was nothing juicy. Then he just pretended to stare at his phone as he looked sideways over the corner of it to see if he could get a glimpse of the blonde's screen. She scrolled through her own feeds in-between hesitant sips from her steaming americano, then opened up an eReader app. She was in the middle of reading *In a Lonely Place* by Dorothy Hughes.

Even with only a glimpse of her screen the excitement of a possible new catch drove him to scan for her data using the Celluracity app. If he could determine which phone was hers amidst the others on the subway he might just be able to install a RAT—a Remote Access Toolkit—on her cell; it was just one of the many little games Chad played to keep himself amused.

He caught whiffs of his fellow travelers' data as the subway bored below the surface of the city, past the access tunnels, past blocked-off entrances from abandoned lines, over and under pipes, fiber optics, and gas lines, and beneath it all, the sewer. He hoped her stop wasn't before his, as he poked around inside a few different phones that weren't hers. He rooted around inside their image folders like a hungry rodent. It was the quickest way to figure out whose phone was whose. When he did log in to her phone, she didn't have as many selfies he'd hoped, but he did find a text from what appeared to be her new employer: *It's great to have you on board Zealia! My wife is going on a girls-only trip next week and I could really use some extra help around here then. I'll pay you overtime. No need to mention it to my wife. She's stressed out enough as it is! ;) ;) ;)*

The text had been sent an hour ago and the blonde, Zealia, still hadn't replied. Her phone *could* hold his interest. It never hurt to have an extra account ratted for his viewing pleasures. He ran the code that gave him discreet access to all her digital activity.

With her accounts now breached, he slipped his cell back into his pocket, though he felt twitchy without ready access to the touchscreen. Then he noticed how hot the back of his neck felt, so hot it was moist with sweat. He wondered if he'd gotten a bug, and then he got the sense someone was watching him and he turned and saw the musician woman, her thick leg up on the seat in front of her, looking at him with concentration. He got his phone back out and started surfing the web for anything that might tantalize him, creeped out by the way the lady stared.

A few minutes later his phone died in his hands. Faint traces of electricity fizzed like soda and then went flat as a swollen point of light on the touch surface sucked everything into a black screen of death. The lights blinked out in the compartment and the raw screech of steel wheels on steel tracks deafened the air. A rumble came from above. As the subway decelerated he fell into Zealia, knocking her phone out of one hand and her tall americano out of the other. The hot coffee splashed across the aisle into the faces of the children, who screamed.

Then he was on top of her and pretended to struggle to get up from the floor where they both had fallen and with the chaos of the screaming kids, used the opportunity to cop a quick fumbled feel of her breast.

"Get your hands off me, you creep!" she yelled as she struggled to push him up and off.

He stumbled up and backwards and felt the hard wheels of a skateboard press into his back as his eyes adjusted to the new dark.

"I'm very sorry," Chad said, "I didn't mean to touch you ... I fell. I'm ... I'm so sorry. I'm very, very, sorry."

"Here, let me help you up," the gruff husband said to the lady. He looked like an old-time strong man in his tight red T-shirt, thick mustache, and meaty arm with a Mom tattoo. His rail-thin husband calmed their kids, and wiped off the excess coffee with a shirt. The compartment was saturated with the earthy aroma of roasted beans.

The coffee had been hot, but the kids weren't scalded and they settled down into a nervous mumble that mimicked the startled emotions of the adults.

She turned to the kids. "I'm sorry about getting the coffee on you."

One of the fathers asked, "Are you okay?"

She shook her head and turned to Chad. "I was okay until you pawed me."

"Chill out lady, it was an accident," Chad said, and then he felt the end of the teenager's skateboard press against his back.

"Accident, my ass," the musician said from the back. Her voice was husky as if it had been honed singing lounge music in the speakeasies where dissidents drank and smoked and gathered in numbers larger than the state allowed. "You were creeping on her ever since we got on this train. After you checked your stalker-drone feeds and the social media accounts you stalk, you hacked her phone."

Chad let out a snort and uneasy laugh, shocked she knew what he'd done. "That's crazy talk and you'd all be crazy to believe it."

"I *thought* he *was* spying on me!" Zealia said.

"Speaking of phones, mine's dead," the skater said, his board still pressed on Chad.

"Nothing on mine either," said the Asian man.

Other passengers looked at their devices and uttered the same.

"What in the hell happened?" the skater asked.

"Who knows," the musician said and took a stub of a candle out of the inside pocket of her heavy clothes. She struck the match on her teeth and brought the flame to the wick. "Maybe it was an EMP. Maybe it was a terrorist attack. Maybe God got sick of watching us crawl around on this rock and decided to turn out the lights for Western civilization's final act."

The subway car was lit with eerie shadows from the orange glow of her candle. "But here we all are," she continued. "Together and stuck. At least for now. So what do y'all think we should do with this creeper? See, I know he hacked her. I knew exactly what he was doing. And still, some people can't get enough of 6G, talking about how great it is. All it's good for is Big Brother and pervs like this guy who want to watch someone's every move!"

Chad gave her a look and shuddered. In the candle light he could swear her fur coat was alive. That it moved. He was having a rough time coming to terms with the fact that some street scum, some bag lady from the way she smelled, some freak musician, knew he had hacked the blonde.

"How do you know he hacked me?" Zealia was angry and amazed. It felt true.

"I didn't!" Chad said.

The skater moved in front of him and threatened him with his deck. "Get on over in your own corner, away from her, away from the kids, away from everybody."

Chad rubbed his eyebrows, sighed, looked down at his Ferragamo shoes, so polished they reflected the flames from the musician's candle. "Fine. Let's just all mind our own business here, okay. Who knows how long it will be before power gets restored and the subway gets moving."

"I'll mind my own business as soon as I see that my phone isn't compromised, that you don't have access to my data."

"You're going to have to get a search warrant or something if you want to look at my phone. You can't just demand to see my private information!"

The musician let out a rasping laugh. "That's real rich, real, real rich coming from a bona fide stalker like you."

"When we get out of this you're gonna be sure I'm going to the police," Zealia yelled, her pustule of rage having burst.

"Are we going to be in here forever, daddy?" one of the kids asked.

"No, no, it'll be alright. The power will get restored. They have backup generators. Don't worry, we'll get moving. They'll think of something."

"Except what if they don't?" the musician said back. "Think of something, that is. What if this is just the way things are now?"

The commuters muttered, wondered who she was, some wondered *what* she was, yet they all seemed to know deep in their under-mind that she did hold authority and ought to be listened to. They all seemed to notice the fur coat she wore was alive and moved. Rodents, some with red fur, some with brown, all with prehensile tails, and moving black fur that glinted with an oily sheen in the light from the wax nub that sputtered and dripped, hot, over her wrinkled hands and thumbs.

She looked much older now than she had on the platform.

Chad reached inside his suit jacket pocket and rested one hand on the X42P Pulse Taser he kept there, crossed the other.

A distraught man from the next compartment banged on the glass window of the door between them. The Asian man got up, tried to pull open the doors, before giving up in exasperation.

Zealia introduced herself to the couple and kids.

"I'm Clara," said the little girl. "And I'm Jim," said her brother.

Zealia knelt down next to them and started to play. It was the best thing she could do to distract herself. She felt nauseous, first from her new boss with his insinuations and now this guy; if she dwelled on it she'd retch.

"My people will be here soon," the musician said. "Anybody who wants out of this sardine can is free to go back up top, or come with us."

No one knew what to believe. It all seemed improbable to them still. Time drifted in the relative silence of their shared heavy breathing, the whispers of their shared anxiety.

Zealia helped Jim and Clara push a little race car, a blue Hot Wheels Model S Tesla, on the floor. Jim pushed it too hard and it ran into Chad, scuffed his polished shoe.

He bent down, picked up the toy, and stepped forward, his other hand still on the Taser.

"Stop! Don't move any closer," Zealia said.

"Just put the car down and push it back over," the gruff father said.

"I'm not doing anything, I was just going to bring your kid his toy." He took another step.

The skater was up, his deck raised. "Don't move or this skateboard's gonna smash your face!"

"Go to hell, punk," and he pulled out the Taser and fired, only it just clicked. Nothing happened. Whatever electrical charge it once held was gone. The gun was limp, just like Chad.

Footsteps could be heard on top of the subway, just as the skater cracked Chad with the board. Chad dodged just enough to take the hit on his shoulder, which throbbed as he dropped his weapon.

"Here they come," the musician said.

The beefcake husband got up, grabbed Chad's arms, and twisted them into a hold behind his back.

Crowbars clanked against the steel and the door opened. Thirteen men and women poured in. They all looked ragged and ratty like the musician, their faces caked with the black dust of the subway tunnels.

The head of one was tilted at a strange angle, as if his cramped neck was always bent, and wild wisps of red hair tufted out from the holes in his nuclear-green beanie cap. "Oi! Howdy Momma!" he said and walked up to the musician and gave her a hug. "We finally made it for ya."

"Ahh, my children, my family, I knew you'd come for me. Augusto, would you mind helping restrain that man there? I think we'll be taking him home with us. People of the subway car, meet my family."

"The Bremen Fremen Family, that's what you can call us," Augusto said with pride as he took some rope out of a pocket and cinched Chad as tight as he'd ever been bound.

Chad whimpered in his bonds as the strange clan took control of the situation. The musician they called *Momma* directed a gnomish-looking lady who wore sweatpants and a floppy bright green wizard hat to take anyone who wanted to leave up a service walkway back to the surface. The couple and their kids, the skateboarder, and everyone else in the car made a quick exodus, along with people from the other cars who were all in varying states of wonder and panic.

Zealia straggled around as the others left, weirded out by all the events. She wanted to get Chad's phone and make sure he had no access to her internet profiles, take it to the cops.

She looked at Momma, "Can I get his cell? I'm going to expose this bastard."

"He'll get justice, don't you worry, hon. My family will see to that. You can come along and watch if ya want. It might make ya feel better! But I'm afraid whatever dirty little secrets he had on that thing are toast, along with all the data in every NSA server farm, all the digital records in all the banks, everything. Boom. It's been wiped clean, baby. Y2K ain't got nothing on how quiet this event has made the world. Which is to say darling, whatever he had on his phone ain't gonna matter one lick."

A vein on Chad's forehead flickered as he seethed. "This is bullshit. The cloud has backups, they've got generators, and who knows what else. Once the power comes back on, and it always does, they'll be coming down here looking for your ratfink asses."

Momma chuckled, "Ratfink. That's good. You don't know how right you are, Chad. Momma Ratty, that's one of the names my boys and girls call me."

"How'd you know my name?"

"I know lots of things."

"I still want his cell," Zealia said, annoyed.

So Momma fished it out and gave it to her as Chad squirmed.

"Let's get back to the rat nest."

The group pushed and pulled Chad along through the web of tunnels that was the city subway system. Zealia had always been fascinated with blogs and online channels devoted to urban exploring, but it was something she never thought she'd get to do herself—but here she was, going through the silent dark, with a group of weirdos even more eccentric than those she'd hung around when she was nineteen during her brief stint in art school.

August started talking as they walked. "See, Momma here, she taught us how to ride the worm. Or what you folken up top call the sub*way*. She been prophesying about the death of the worm for some time here now. She said when the worm died the 'lectricity would die too. And she done told the truth."

"The electricity will come back on," Chad said.

"Naw it won't," Augusto said.

"Yes it will," Chad argued.

"Naw it won't. I'll prove it. Go ahead now and put your foot on the third rail. Ya ain't a yellowbellied chicken are ya?"

Chad's fancy footwear was even more scuffed than before. What did he have to lose? The electricity was off now, even if it would come back on, once the right people figured things out. He felt a knife jab in his back, and heard Augsto say, "Do it ya chicken." Then he set the heel of his shoe on the third rail. He tried to control his racing heart, his fear, as he set his foot down, and felt relieved when he didn't get juiced.

"All that proves is the electric is out. It'll come back on." Yet in the back of

Chad's mind he wondered if it wouldn't come back on this time. What would happen to all the dollars he'd invested in crypto?

"Mayhap that was true in the past, but this here is the end of all that," Augusto said.

"Augusto speaks the truth," Momma said.

Zealia didn't know what to believe.

They walked the rest of the way through the decrepit tunnels until they reached a large space that had once housed heavy equipment, lit with oil lamps, torches and candles. Remains of old machines littered the floor and the Bremen Fremen Family who'd stayed behind lounged about on moth-chewed furniture. Everything and everyone was assembled from the bric-a-brac of society's discards and castaways.

"Make yourself comfortable," Augusto said to her.

She looked around. Besides it being in the subway it looked like any one of the crusty punk squatter houses she'd gone to see bands play in back in her wild days. In one corner was a drum kit and array of acoustic instruments. There was a large bookshelf with a bunch of pulp and sci-fi novels. *Garbage World* by Charles Platt sat next to a stained copy of Sol Yurick's *The Warriors* and *City of Darkness* by Ben Bova. There were multiple copies of all of the *Dune* books by Frank Herbert.

"Augusto, get Chad's shoes and clothes, divide them up amongst yourselves and then put him in the cage," Momma said with a casual air.

Chad looked incredulous and defeated.

Augusto did as Momma bade. The Family squabbled over his shoes and underwear. Augusto took his smart pinky ring; he wanted to use it in his septum piercing.

The rusted cage was tall and they forced him into it at the ends of curved shortswords they pulled out from scabbards hidden beneath their baggy homeless-looking getups. Inside he banged around as his mind rattled. The Family hoisted it up on a long chain and pulley attached to the concrete ceiling.

"Open the rat pit," Momma said.

Two ladies opened an access door the cage had sat on. From it emerged a ferocious cacophony of squeaks, and the stink of sewage.

"This is my personal rat pit," Momma said. "I find it comes in useful when people don't cooperate. It opens straight into the city sewer and we found that if we just toss in some meat every now and then we always have plenty of rats."

Chad pleaded "Please, please don't kill me, don't hurt me. I'll do anything you want, just let me get out of here. I promise I'll stop stalking people. I promise."

Momma pointed to the Family who worked the pulley. They lowered the cage closer to the rat pit. A steaming golden liquid that smelled of ammonia and fear spilled out of the cage and into the pit as Chad lost control of his bladder.

"Can I get out of here, now?" Zealia asked. "I don't really need to stay and watch this. I've got his phone..." She was afraid this kind of justice would end in his death and didn't want that on her conscience.

Momma's eyes probed Zealia. "You ain't afraid are ya? Fear is the mind killer."

Zealia shook her head. "I shall not fear," she found herself saying from some deep part of her.

"Very good," Momma nodded and turned her attention back to Chad.

"Let us now proceed with the interrogation. Why do you spy on women? Is that how you get your jollies off?"

"I..., I..." he cried. When he didn't answer right away the cage was lowered down another rung, closer to the pit where the rats leapt out and nipped at his clean feet and clean skin.

Hoping to avoid being dropped further into the pit he said, "I don't know why I do it. I just started one day, and I got away with it. Then I tried again, and I couldn't stop. I wanted to quit, but I always found another excuse, and then I forgot about wanting to quit. It just escalated."

"Fair enough," Momma said. "Now don't you feel better for having confessed? Perhaps there are some other weights that have been dangling around your neck that you'd like to let go of."

He cowered in the back corner of the cage and it leaned back closer to the rats and they nibbled at his delicate flesh with their long yellow teeth and red tongues.

Momma made a motion to lower him down another notch and he started talking of his creepy crimes, of hacking women's accounts, of the ways he'd manipulated women online through hacking their friends' and lovers' accounts to go to places where he could watch them, make moves and advances on them. Of the drones he used to watch them. Of the girls and models he hired to photograph for his amateur porno site. And he sobbed and cried like a pathetic wretch as he told them.

"Okay, I've heard enough," Momma said. "Drop him all the way down and then we'll play some music."

The cage splashed into the sewage goop and the rats started to crawl all around it, skittering and nibbling at his flesh. Momma took her squeezebox and started playing a high-pitched drone, while Augusto got on the drums, and others picked up and started playing whatever was around in a ferocious racket of engulfing noise that went on for what seemed like an hour to Zealia, and hours and hours to Chad, but was only about twenty-three minutes in total clock time. Chad thrashed with the rats in his own private hell, a kind of moshpit, with nothing to bang against except his steel cage, the noise of all the musicians a roaring din as the world above had gone silent.

Then they stopped all at once and raised him out of the pit. Chad was caked in a bulbous and gritty grey-black slime. There were bite marks and scratches on all of his skin. He was worried about going septic, about disease.

"Spray him off and take him through Face Dancer Tunnel, as he is, naked, and put him up through the grate that leads out into the main square. He can make his way home or wherever he needs to go from there," Momma commanded.

Chad gave Zealia and all of them a look of dazed hatred as he was rinsed of the grime in one of their storm water showers. When a group of them led him out the tunnel Zealia flipped him the bird and spat on the floor.

Then she sat down on the couch, exhausted. Momma talked to her and helped her calm down, and then told her of how she'd started the Family after losing her job as a music teacher during a round of layoffs seven years ago, of how one drifting musician, homeless and out of work, running low on hope, connected with her in the streets, and how they'd found the space in the tunnel; how they had all come with a copy of one of the *Dune* books by Frank Herbert, and how those stories shaped the evolving Bremen Fremen Family philosophy.

"Why don't you stay here tonight?" Momma asked.

"Sure, okay. I'm *way* late for my job now. I was pretty much just gonna quit anyway."

Momma made up a couch for her to sleep on with soft wool blankets and a down pillow. It took her a while, but she finally fell asleep. The next morning she woke up as if it had all been a crazy dream, but it wasn't; she was still beneath the city, in the Family nest.

"Can I go home now?"

"Yes, but remember us, and what I told of things to come."

"I will, I promise. Thank you, for getting me off the subway, for getting his phone, for giving him justice, for everything."

"You're welcome. Come back and visit us sometime."

"If I can, I will."

Then Augusto led her up through a maze of tunnels to the subway station near Hillside and Fenton, close to where she lived. As she clambered out of a utility grate her eyes squinted from the brightness of the morning sun.

Most urbanites will recognize that walking past four closed coffee shops on a Friday morning is a sure sign of apocalypse. So when Zealia found herself walking past them without their lines, and past the empty offices and the empty stores, one after another, a strange feeling settled over her. A feeling of peace when she looked up at the security cameras and saw she wasn't being watched, a feeling of serenity when she looked at the large screen that had been mounted to the side of the One World Bank tower. Its endless parade of talking heads had been silenced. The voices that chattered and the relentless advertisements had disappeared, for the better, she thought.

In place of the silence something else had emerged, a voice still small to her scattered mind. It was working its way up to being heard, so long stifled by the everyday riot of living at high speed. Now it had a chance.

When Zealia saw the pile of cellphones surrounding a lamppost outside the Drake Hotel, she smiled. Someone had spray painted GOODNIGHT BIG BROTHER! on the street in front of the silicon reliquary.

She stopped at it and stared. She held Chad's phone in her hand, looked at it, and thought of the secrets of her life it had compromised. She chucked it onto the pile. Then she dug into her pocket and pulled out her own inert phone. She stared at its blank screen and smiled as she tossed it onto the grave of other dead cells.

Her feet carried her in the direction of home and as she walked she thought she could hear notes of squeezebox music drifting up from the grates of the sewers on the otherwise quiet streets.

David Crawford

Way Out

"You sure this is the place?" asked Vishinski suspiciously, leaning forward from the rear seat of the limousine.

"It's the address your secretary gave me," said Tariq from behind the armored glass partition.

Vishinski hesitated. The house was like a hundred others in Chelsea, with only a street number on the door. It certainly wasn't the restaurant he'd been expecting. On the other hand, Tariq usually knew what he was talking about when it came to addresses, and most other things as well, actually. He had been a pediatric surgeon in the Gulf before the New Oil Wars, after which there was little need for surgeons of any kind, except to patch up the wounded. He had wandered the Arab world for some years, dodging bombs and revolutions, before eventually coming to America as an illegal immigrant.

Vishinski had found him driving an unlicensed taxi, and hired him on the spot. He preferred illegals, partly because they were cheaper, but mostly because of the feeling of power and control that it gave him. Tariq knew that with one phone call, and "Frankly officer, I had no idea!" he could rapidly find himself in Guantánamo having his fingernails pulled out, even though he was from an old Iraqi Christian family.

On the other hand, Tariq spoke perfect English and had total recall of New York's streets, more than ever necessary in this era when smartphones were no longer reliable, so he would keep him on for at least a little bit longer. And as he looked at his watch, he realized it was two minutes to the hour. Good thing he had allowed an hour for the two-mile journey: there had been another power failure, and the traffic lights were out again. Maybe he should buy a horse and carriage, just becoming fashionable again? At least the pavement wasn't covered in bird shit like before. Where were the birds these days anyway? He'd find out when he had a moment.

"Let me out," he said. Tariq jumped out to open the rear door, and Vishinski stepped into the murderous, record-breaking October heat. Across the road, oblivious to the blinding sun, were a group of bald men and women in white robes holding up signs saying THE SAUCERS WILL SAVE US. He had just decided that if this was all a set-up he would fire Tariq, and fire his secretary as well, when the door opened and a distinguished-looking black major-domo gazed benignly down at him from the top of the steps. "Good afternoon Mr. Vishinski, Mr. Stahlman is expecting you," he said, his voice polished smooth by years of servility.

Stahlman, he thought, mounting the stairs towards the front door and gratefully entering the air-conditioned building. (Why was air-conditioning much rarer than it used to be? He supposed it must be a fuel thing). He followed the major-domo down what seemed to be just the hall of an ordinary house, except for closed doors on either side, from behind which there came the faint murmur of voices, and the tinkling of cutlery.

Stahlman, he thought again. A legend among Wall Street legends. Stahlman and Bronstein had been around for so long that they had become part of the furniture of American history. Stahlman himself, like his father and grandfather, had moved frictionlessly from running one of the world's major merchant banks to helping to run the American government, and back again. He had been Secretary of the Treasury, and was currently the chair of a Presidential Task Force on bank deregulation, when he wasn't running the bank itself.

The major-domo opened the door into a long, narrow, rather gloomy room with a single table at the end, by a set of full-length windows. Stahlman was sitting there, silhouetted against the light, talking into a mobile telephone which somehow looked as if it was made of solid gold: perhaps it was; only the wealthy could afford decent ones now, since supplies of rare earths were cut off by the wars, and the chips were hard to find.

Vishinski had always hated Stahlman as a matter of principle, with the kind of pure, exterminatory hatred of the newly rich for those for whom wealth had long been an entirely virtual concept. He doubted that Stahlman had ever put his hand in his pocket to pay for anything in his life. Now he had a chance to hate him in person, dressed as he was in a suit that probably cost as much as Vishinski's Porsche, but which Vishinski could never have worn without feeling intimidated by it.

"Tell him that he does what we want and he gets the money, or that he doesn't do what we want and he doesn't get the money," said Stahlman in the kind of voice you use for talking to children and servants. (He was reputed to own at least three Senators outright, and to have a partial interest in another ten.)

For want of anything better to do, Vishinski sat down on the other side of the table, which was set with expensive silver cutlery. There was a silver decanter full of water and, feeling brave, he poured himself some. It seemed to have come out of a tap.

After several more gnomic but threatening remarks, Stahlman put his phone down and, as if by magic, a formally attired waiter appeared with two bowls of something that looked like the water left after an intensive washing-up session, and a plate of wafer biscuits. Stahlman made no move to eat, and spoke at, rather than to, Vishinski as he was flicking through the messages on his phone. He spoke in the unattractive rasping monotone that Vishinski remembered from his public appearances.

"So you've heard of global warming," he said. "Everybody has. Probably you think it's all a con, or at least it's exaggerated. That's what we want you to think. Actually, it's not what you imagine, it's worse than that. A lot worse." He paused to do something to a message and adjusted his cuff. The suit seemed to sparkle, as though it was honoured to be worn by him. "We've been working for a long time now to get reports suppressed, stop the really bad news from getting out, because if people get frightened, they'll demand government action, and that will mean more taxes. That's not in anyone's interest." He stirred the colourless liquid in his bowl without taking any. "And most of the, you know, valuable metals and so on are running out, but we've managed to keep that away from the plebs. Apparently those chip things are only made in Taiwan now, and that earthquake last year took most of them out, I didn't know that. De-industrialisation, they call it, somebody told me yesterday. You've probably read about how technology will save us. Wrong, it's gone too far now, though we pay for books and TV and so on to make people think differently. Whatever. All of it, it's going to get a lot worse very quickly." He shrugged. "People like us, we're protected for a while, but even we can't avoid it forever.

"So of course we've been thinking of a way out, and you can imagine the kind of thing we've been thinking about. For a while we had people look at desert islands, and after that some remote mountain area in Russia or China or whatever. But if you take a decent-sized community, say 500 people, then you need about three or four times that many plebs before life becomes bearable. Somebody has to grow the food, clean the houses, provide security, all that stuff, and then you're into a lot of people. Apparently it wouldn't be self-sustaining, and anyway there's this resource shortage thing. Plus you don't want lots of men with guns around, because they might get the wrong ideas about who's in control." He pushed the soup bowl away. Vishinski tried a little of the liquid, which did indeed taste like washing-up water. He pushed his away as well. The wafers were dry and tasteless.

"So we had to look around for something else, and, guess what, that something else found us?" Again, as if by some kind of magic, the waiter appeared again behind Vishinski's shoulder and took the two bowls away.

"I had a lot of trouble believing this and if I hadn't seen it with my own eyes like you're going to, then I probably would have said it was a load of garbage. But I am who I am, and you are who you are, so when I say believe, you believe. Anyway, we've made contact with aliens from somewhere, I'm not sure where, exactly, who think pretty much like we do, and they're going to let us buy our way off this planet."

I'm in a lunatic asylum, thought Vishinski and this man isn't who he says he is. He's some kind of religious maniac. Otherwise it's some kind of reality television and I'm the victim. He tried to get up, or at least look around, but when Stahlman raised his eyes and looked at him, he realised that it was in fact the famous Joseph Stahlman sitting opposite him, and that he was deadly serious. They both ignored the colourless things on expensive china placed before them by the waiter, that might once have been a type of fish.

"You'll get all the details when you come to Tokyo next month. You're going to cancel all your engagements and my people will tell your people where to go and where to meet." He paused. "But basically what we are looking for is investors, people who have a lot of liquid cash and a good trading instinct. I've never been much good at the, you know, banking side of banking, but I can recognize a good numbers man when I see one. That's why you'll be in Tokyo. The way it's going to work, a group of alien traders are coming to this system in a few years time. They're not supposed to be here, actually, because we haven't been officially contacted or something yet, but they're the kind of people who don't pay too much attention to fussy rules that get in the way of business. The reason they're interested in us is, gold. Apparently, I didn't know this, gold is one of the rarest elements in the universe, and their home planet doesn't have any at all. A bar of gold, and you're the equivalent of a billionaire in their system. They're going to take us off this planet, take a percentage in gold, and re-settle us wherever we like. With the sort of net worth you've got, you can buy an entire planet. Literally, I mean."

A numbers, man, well, he was that all right. His grandfather had been a famous physicist and one of the fathers of the Soviet space program. One day, he had told his young grandson, we will solve all our problems in this world, and travel to the planets. We've outgrown religion, he would say: now science alone can save us. He had a tattered collection of brightly illustrated comics showing Soviet cosmonauts on Mars. His parents were both computer scientists who had started by working for Gosplan, out of a job when Yeltsin destroyed the Russian economy. From desperation, they went to work for the *Mafiya*, helping to funnel loans from the World Bank into the foreign bank accounts of Russian oligarchs. But then his father became greedy, and as a result he became stupid, and started to skim money off into an account of his own. What he didn't know, was there was a team of even better qualified programmers watching his parents. They came for his father, and there wasn't enough left to be worth burying. But they left the money, as a gesture of contempt as much as anything else.

Undaunted, his mother emptied the account, and what remained of the family fled the country. Palms were greased to provide them with residence in the U.S., and Vishinski was seen through school and college. His grandfather died a few years after they arrived, of a broken heart, pretty much. His mother yearned to go back to Russia, but even under Putin it was too dangerous. She didn't so much die, as just fade away slowly, until there was nothing. He realized she must be gone when several weeks passed, and she didn't call him.

Vishinski had been reading mathematics at university when he'd suddenly realized one day how little mathematics most economists actually knew. There was more money in economics, he realized, but there was even more money, lots of money in fact, in fake economics. With a freshly minted doctorate, using mathematics that his examiners could hardly understand, let alone evaluate, he went off in search of the fortune he thought he was entitled to. He considered an academic career for about five minutes, before joining a merchant bank, then a bigger one, then a hedge fund, and finally opening his own, developing along the way a bottomless contempt for people who bought stocks and shares in anything, in the hope of becoming rich. He employed a few people to wine and dine the customers with their own money, while he designed simple algorithms to rob them, and make them feel grateful for being robbed.

"You'll be there in Tokyo," said Stahlman, pushing his plate away and picking up his phone. It was not a question.

As the door opened, he glanced at his watch: he could still afford a digital one. Fifteen minutes? It had seemed much longer. Or maybe shorter. He didn't feel particularly bad about being treated like shit: everybody in his world treated the weaker party like shit; it was expected. He'd take it out on somebody later. And there was the money. And deliverance from a world which, even he realized, was coming to an end. Speaking of taking it out, Tariq had better be there. And he was. He had been studying the lyrics of songs by Lou Reed recently, and was frowning over *The Black Angel's Death Song* on the limousine's video player.

Somebody's people had booked the restaurant on the twenty-fifth floor of the New Otani Hotel. If it hadn't been raining so heavily you could have seen the Imperial Palace, thought Vishinski. Nobody was sure whether the weather was this year's rainy season come very late, or next year's come very early. Outside the restaurant was a statue of a fierce-looking god: Raijin, one of the waiters said, we're praying to him for the end of the rain. As it was, you couldn't see further than the rank of electronic taxi rickshaws in the street below. The room was full of hard-faced men and women, walking around and doing things powerful, important people did, mostly involving telephones. (The hotel had its own telephone mast.) Somebody was apparently firing her personal assistant by text message. Somebody else was screaming at his divorce lawyer. Stahlman was standing at a banquet table looking even more beatific than usual, watching things and people arrange themselves to please him, as they had all his life. One of his people whispered deferentially into his ear, and slid away, taking a crowd of hangers-on and spear-carriers with him.

Vishinski happened to look away for a moment and then suddenly, out of the corner of his eye, saw that something had appeared. Where there had been nothing, there was an object. It was vaguely humanoid, with a black, metallic appearance, and it was sitting calmly on a chair just next to Stahlman. A wave of silence, with an undercurrent of fear, spread out from the table all around the room as people turned, looked, and stopped whatever they were doing. "I'll call you back," whispered the man who had been shouting at his lawyer.

"We have a visitor," said Stahlman. "He is a messenger from the starship *Parousia*, which, apparently, means something in their language, he'll explain. It's still several, ah, years' travel away from Earth." At that, the newcomer raised one human-looking right hand, and in the air before them appeared a black deltoid shape barely visible against a background of stars.

"This is the *Parousia*," said a voice that seemed not to come from the being itself, but from every solid surface in the room at the same time. "In our language, it means something like 'visiting merchant.' It will be in your system in about three years. The ship has room to take about five hundred people as passengers in some comfort, so we are looking for two hundred fifty investors from this planet, together with their partners. We cannot take any children. Those of you who can contribute the most gold to the total will get the best choice of facilities on the ship, and the first choice of investments when we arrive. Any of you, with the gold you now own, has more net worth than any citizen of our civilization. You will be the equivalent of kings and queens. But ..." There was a silence, the kind that comes just before the descent of the executioner's axe. "I cannot emphasize enough how sensitive this project is. The crew expect to make enough money from it to retire, but it is completely illegal and the penalties for them if they are discovered are severe." Pause. "We will be recruiting the investors progressively, and each of them will be sworn to absolute secrecy. For the moment, you must tell no one of your plans. Not even your closest family. If any of you withdraw from the project later, you are sworn to secrecy for the rest of your life. Six months before the project is complete, you can nominate one companion, and that person must go with you. If they are unwilling to go, they will be killed. If they tell anyone else both of them will be killed. Too much is at stake here to worry about ethics."

There was a rustling and murmuring throughout the room. The messenger leaned forward and opened a box, which had not been there a moment before.

"Of course, some of you will doubt me," it said. "So here is a trivial example of our technology. It is a small nano-engineering device, like a pill. If you take it today, and then every fourth Wednesday, then for a month the nano-machines will travel around your body healing everything. In principle, if you have a good supply of these pills, and in our society you will, then you will live forever. Each of you will be given such a box before you leave."

The room was utterly silent now: people who thought they were Masters and Mistresses of the Universe had just seen the actual Universe. They turned and looked at each other for unexpected and unfamiliar things like support and comfort. Stahlman picked up a tiny capsule from the box and popped it into his mouth with a broad smile. "I've been taking these for five years myself now," he chuckled, "and my doctor can't understand why I'm getting younger and not older."

And then, between two heartbeats, the messenger was gone, and only the box remained. "Jesus Christ!" said somebody. It was almost a prayer.

Sutcliffe awoke, and as usual was surprised to find himself not dead. More than that, he was in a bed. Most of his mornings recently had started with him waking up face-down on the floor, in the bedroom or in the toilet, and usually covered in vomit. But this morning was different, and it took him a while to understand why. Then he looked around and saw that his clothes had been neatly folded over a chair, and that he was even wearing the hotel's sleeping outfit. He twisted around and looked at the bedside clock. It was just after 8 in the morning, which for somebody who was usually blitzed by a combination of alcohol, cocaine, insomnia and jet-lag at that hour, was absolutely amazing.

There was something else as well, although he couldn't immediately place it. Right. He actually felt okay. He felt rested, almost as though he had slept all night through. Actually, he had. He lay in bed trying to work out why, after all these months, years even, he now felt approximately human for once, almost as if he had been reborn. Then he remembered the pill that he had taken the afternoon before. He hadn't thought much about it at the time, assumed it was all sales talk. He'd been out and got drunk as usual, although this time he remembered coming back to the hotel before midnight, still with his wallet in his pocket, and without having thrown up between the taxi and the hotel front door. Then he remembered something about going up to his room, and actually going to bed in something like a normal fashion. Yes, it could only have been this pill that he taken yesterday. What was he going to do today?

It had been a long time since Sutcliffe had really thought about the future, even about later on the same day. Well-meaning people, some of whom wanted his job, told him that, even at his age, it was time to retire. He had made more money than he could count, let alone spend, and it was time to go off and do something interesting. The fact was, though, that there was nothing he was interested in, not even making more money: he hated the environment, hated the people, and was bored to death except when he was actually doing the trading. There, the mixture of fear, greed and uncertainty actually made him feel reasonably alive, at least for a while. But he was also brutally aware that there was nothing else he could actually *do*. In some ways, and for all his money, he was just as boring a person as his hated father had been: a wholesale butcher in a slimy market town in Yorkshire, spending his days haggling in markets over the price of meat.

Sutcliffe's father had beaten him a lot, not because he had done anything wrong, but just as a way of demonstrating his power over him, the same way he beat his wife. Sutcliffe accepted this as normal until the day he realized he was bigger and stronger than his father. The next time his father raised a hand, Sutcliffe beat the living shit out of him, leaving him bleeding and mewling on the floor. That had been decades ago, and he had no idea whether his father was still alive: he couldn't be bothered to find out, anyway.

He left school and got a job working for a bookmaker, where his natural flair for numbers was finally of some use. He became a gambler and poker player, and made a decent living from a strange combination of a photographic memory for numbers and a barely controlled aggression. After all that, a move into trading, and lots of money, was more or less inevitable, through somebody who owed him a gambling debt he couldn't repay. But for all that, Sutcliffe knew that wasn't an interesting person. He had very little education, and virtually no culture. He didn't read books and knew very little about music, and not many other people were interested in his definitive collection of 1980s kung fu movies. He hated working, but if he stopped working he would die of boredom or something worse, within a few months. He tried to forget about how much he hated himself and his work by drinking himself insensible in the evenings, and had to rely on cocaine to get him through the next working day. He knew that he was slowly killing himself, but there was no other way that he could see of staying alive.

Even among traders, he had a name for being difficult and even unpleasant. Women were attracted briefly to his wealth, but repelled by his habits and his personality. The fact was, he was doing the one job he could do, and the job that he was superlatively good at. He hated that job, but it was all that there was in his life.

He lay back on the pillow and started to think for a moment. Maybe this weird idea had something in it after all. Maybe escaping from this dying planet, turning all his assets into gold, and then, who knew, buying an entire planet to play with, would actually give him something to live for, for a change? To his surprise, he found himself swinging his legs out of bed and heading for the shower. Life might turn out to be a lot more rewarding than he had thought possible when he shambled, still half drunk, off the flight from London the day before.

It had been raining steadily in London for three days now: a heavy, incessant, tropical monsoon rain that drove cars and buses off the road. Heathrow Airport had been closed since noon the day before. Vishinski's plane from Johannesburg had been the last one to land successfully, lurching and bouncing as it hit a runway that was almost completely flooded, and for the first time in a long while he had actually been physically afraid. He looked through the window of his hotel room at a curtain of rain that seemed eternal and inexhaustible, as if it could wash the whole world away. He could not remember the name of his hotel: they all looked the same, even the executive suites. But then he was lucky: mere Business Class travellers were sleeping on the seats in the Terminals, and at least his hotel had its own generator. (What was this Eco crap about flying being a luxury for the rich now?) His connecting flight to New York was delayed indefinitely, just like all the other flights to everywhere else. And the weather seemed to be getting worse, rather than better: every now and then the wind hammered against the window like some angry Hollywood monster, and the whole room seem to shake.

"I hope you realize how disappointed I am," Amy was saying on the telephone. Reception was not good — it never was, these days — but he could clearly hear the anger in her voice. "I really wanted to go to the opera tonight. Extracts from the *Götterdämmerung*. Wagner. You've heard of that, haven't you?"

"Look," said Vishinski with the willingness of someone who is being held like a hostage, "I didn't organize this weather, you know, and I was supposed to be back yesterday afternoon. I'm sorry about the opera, but can't you ask one of your family to go?"

"For God's *sake*," snapped Amy, "what am I supposed to say when they ask me where you are? You never come to the opera with me, you always have some kind of excuse for being somewhere else."

"You tell them to switch on the TV and watch the news about London. That's the bit in the south of the country to the left of Europe. I'll get back to you when I've got some news," said Vishinski wearily.

"Don't break your neck," said Amy, cutting the connection.

He put the phone down, and as he did so the wind delivered a spectacular kick to the side of the hotel, which rattled the windows and made all the furniture in the room shudder. He wondered when, if ever, he would actually get on a plane again. He felt like one of those characters in the children's stories his grandmother had read to him: locked in a magic castle, and needing a spell or a supernatural figure to let him out. Which made him think, of course, of immortality, the little magic pills, and the alien spaceship that was going to take him somewhere where he would be, quite literally, a Master of the Universe.

But he wasn't going to take Amy. The idea of spending an effective eternity with her had never been particularly attractive: now it seemed more and more like a really lousy proposition. He had the impression that she, too, was starting to re-evaluate the decision she had made ten years before. On the face of it, it had seemed a good bargain. Old money, social position and property meets new money and fashionable hard-to-understand technologies. "Like a Balzac novel," one of his French colleagues had said. At the time, he thought this was some kind of obscene joke, but he later found out from Google that Balzac was a French novelist.

But although the money was old there was not that much of it. There was the large apartment overlooking Central Park, the house in the Hamptons, and other properties scattered around the region. But it was a struggle to maintain them, and most of the family worked in relatively modest jobs as lawyers or doctors, and made livings that were comfortable enough, but nothing remotely in the same league as him. And soon, it became clear that Amy saw him as the family's financial savior. (She was an ardent feminist, except where money was concerned.) It was always somebody's college fees here, somebody's medical bills there. "We have lots of money," Amy would say, "we should share it with others."

"*I* have lots of money," he would say, unleashing a violent argument. Amy had some kind of trivial job in arts administration, which barely paid for their daughter's school fees. It was time for a change. He'd miss his daughter, he supposed. He supposed.

Perhaps he shouldn't have been surprised about how things had turned out. After all, he couldn't, off-hand, think of anyone he actually liked, or wanted to spend time with, let alone eternity. Back when he had first gone into banking, one of the partners had taken him to lunch in a very expensive and sophisticated French restaurant near the office, to humiliate him. "What you have to understand," the man had said, over coffee, "is that Wall Street is like Hollywood, only worse. Everybody hates everybody else and nobody knows anything. At least over there they produce stuff, even if most of it's shit."

He'd recounted this conversation, jokily, to his mother, not long before she died. After a while, she shook her head, and said, slowly, "A society that doesn't produce anything will wind up consuming itself instead." Vishinski had laughed (he felt awkward about that, later) and he said,"well, okay, as long as I get the last mouthful!" His mother had stared past him, up into the sky.

The windows shook again, as though a giant elephant was trying to kick the hotel over.

The wind over Geneva was particularly strong today, and the airport had been closed since early in the morning. The fountain in the lake had been switched off, and the terrace of the Noga Hilton, where Stangl had expected to meet his victim, had been closed as well. The wind rattled the windows, and occasional gusts blew the curtains around. A flailing end of a curtain caught the corner of a pile of champagne glasses and sent them flying. Waiters rushed over to sweep up the shards from the floor.

He sat at a table in the inside restaurant, fingering the little black ampoule he had been given. At five minutes to midday, he crushed the ampoule in the palm of his hand, and dropped it inconspicuously in a waste bin.

Franck was on time, as you would expect from a Swiss banker. He was a small, fussy man with large glasses, who looked like a suburban accountant. He shook hands, took the chair opposite Stangl, and cleared his throat formally before speaking. He placed his elbows on the table, and his hands together in what looked like the position of prayer.

"I hope you have put my proposition to your principals, and that you have a reply from them," he said, leaning forward expectantly. "I have tried to be reasonable, and I do not see any reason why my very moderate demands should not be quite acceptable. I trust you can tell me that your principals agree to accept them in full, or at the very least agree to negotiate."

"I'm afraid my principals have not changed their opinion," said Stangl. "Once they start making exceptions for one person, they have to make exceptions for everybody. At that point, I have been asked to tell you, things become unmanageable. They cannot agree to your demands, and they do not wish to negotiate."

Franck said nothing for a moment or two and then appeared to raise his eyes to heaven, as though seeking some divine understanding for the stupidity of humanity.

"I thought your principals understood that I can be extremely helpful to them, and that I can also be extremely unhelpful to them. Because of my official position, and because of my private investments, I see a great deal of the gold trading that goes on in the world. If I wish to interfere I can do so. If I wish to facilitate I can do that as well. All I demand in return is a small additional percentage in recognition of my special status. I am not greedy. I do not see why your principals should have any problem with this, and I insist that you return to them, and tell them that I am persisting in my demands. I hope that after further reflection they will agree." He sat back in his chair, a small but determined figure peering at Stangl through his thick glasses.

"I will report as you ask," said Stangl, flicking one fingernail against his untouched cup of coffee. "But I doubt if they will change their minds."

"That," said Franck, "will be their problem, I feel, not mine. I will perhaps make a small, publicly visible, gesture within the next week or two to bring home to them the power that I have in this regard."

They stood up, and shook hands formally again. Stangl watched the Swiss walking fussily towards the door, and reflected that he had killed many men in his time, in all sorts of different ways, but never before by shaking hands with them. With his uncontaminated hand, he took the antidote from his left pocket and swallowed it unobtrusively. Then he went downstairs to the toilets, and washed his hands thoroughly for as long as he could. The nerve poison was already in his system, as it was in Franck's, but at least he could avoid contaminating everyone else he touched. He'd earned a decent hotel and a pleasant evening in Geneva, he thought.

There was no antidote, of course. He died two days later.

Sutcliffe had learned about power early in life. It came from brute force and money. When you have power, other people do what you want. You show your own power by making others do your bidding, no matter how silly or unreasonable that is. Power and obedience. That was all life was, really. So several hundred rich and powerful men and women had been jerked away at short notice to come to Beirut in April, with the threat that if they didn't they could forget about deliverance from the problems of Earth, and eternal life. So, as rich and powerful as they were, they had done as they were told.

He had no idea what Beirut in April was supposed to be like, but everybody was complaining about the unseasonably hot, sultry weather mixed with torrential rain and violent winds. There were no luxury yachts in the Marina now: tourism had gone away and wasn't coming back. Over to the east, they were, very slowly, rebuilding the ruins from the great explosion. The weather reminded him of Bangkok the only time he had been there, or at least the only time he remembered being there.

Power, he thought again. When he was a child, if his father wasn't too hung-over on a Sunday morning, he'd take him to the local Congregationalist Chapel. The preacher there had a favorite theme, almost his only one really, which was that there was this God, and he was a vindictive, ill-tempered, all-powerful bastard, and that if you didn't do exactly what he wanted he'd make you burn in hell forever. The preacher was a carpenter by trade, and he had constructed his own pulpit: to a terrified little boy it seemed to tower up high above everything and everybody. One of the preacher's favorite stories had been about the Centurion who was used to issuing orders, and says to Jesus, "I say to one go, and he goeth," and then Jesus just says, "Follow me," and that's it. All about power, really. Why had he thought of that? Because in his room, among the yellowing shopping brochures, had been an old leaflet about tours to Biblical sites in Lebanon, from the days when it was still safe to visit them, and there were still visitors. People must have seen something in religion, once, he thought vaguely.

Which was ultimately why he was sitting, pointlessly, like everybody else, in a basement conference room at the Phoenicia Hotel, next to a beefy South African called De Kock, whose conversation consisted of saying "Yes-No" and telling everyone how he had played prop-forward for the Durban Sharks rugby team. Sutcliffe had actually been out for a walk the afternoon before (the pills were working) but got lost in the streets behind Omar Daouk, and eventually wandered past a building with a portrait of a bearded man with a turban. "Hezbollah," said the barman that evening, when he told him. "The Party of God."

"What's that?" he had asked.

"How long have you got?" replied the man who, like all Lebanese barmen, was a trained political analyst.

Then things started to happen. Men wearing sunglasses indoors and head-mics cleared the room of stragglers, then locked the doors, and stood guard outside them. Stahlman, seeming even younger, bounced up onto the stage and proudly activated something that was supposed to block all communications in and out. And then, between two blinks of an eye, the messenger or something very like it, was back. Its black skin seemed to ripple as it surveyed the room with its eyeless face. Stahlman opened his mouth to speak, but the messenger cut him off.

"The *Parousia* is about six months out from your solar system," said the chair Sutcliffe was sitting on. "It will enter a parking orbit around Saturn, and will send down a shuttle to collect you on New Year's Day." The messenger raised its hand once more, and this time an image of the sea appeared, which zoomed quickly into a close-up of an island. "This island is five hundred kilometers north of Darwin, and about the same distance south of New Guinea. It has an airbase, unused since the 1960s, but now back in commission as the result of work carried out by a company which Mr. Stahlman has been good enough to establish." The eyeless face turned towards Stahlman, who smiled in acknowledgement.

"The same company has hired air movements experts, who will facilitate the landings and departures of your aircraft. All arrivals and departures must take place between oh-nine hundred and thirteen hundred local time, and that leaves space for about thirty movements. Decide among yourselves who will travel in which plane, but Mr. Stahlman's company has already hired two executive Boeing 737s, one leaving from Singapore and the other from Darwin. Hand baggage only may be taken: everything else can be fabricated on board the ship. After the last aircraft has departed, and all retainers and servants have left, the final tally of gold will be calculated, and the positions will be awarded. The coordinates of the island will be sent to you separately. Now." Pause. "I need hardly remind you what will happen if any of you say a word about this to anyone outside this room. Nominated partners may be informed in June that a journey is anticipated and asked to be available, but that is all. Anyone, including members of your immediate family, who discovers anything about this project will be killed immediately. Mr. Stahlman's bank has organized an efficient group of professionals for this purpose. They believe they will be coming with us, though they do not know the details, and it is important they continue to believe this."

And then, quite suddenly, the black figure was not there any more. Sutcliffe found that his hands were shaking. The room was absolutely still. Everyone seemed paralyzed, until eventually Stahlman stood up, with a visible effort.

"Well," he said, "we have our ... instructions. I suggest we get our people working."

Sutcliffe walked out of the hotel, and dodged across the road, through the Beirut traffic, to the Corniche. It was raining now, but not hard. This is it, he thought. He had already decided not to take anyone with him, and to collect the difference in gold. He had no one he could plausibly bring, but, in the course of an eternal life, surely he would find somebody who would put up with him.

"We've been together for a year and you've only just told me," she spat. "And now you're kidnapping me and taking me on some, some ... flying saucer!"

"Gabriella, I ... it's for your own good, your own protection, I ..."

"Oh right," she said caustically. "Little woman can't understand all the difficult stuff, can she, just stay at home in the kitchen?"

"Gabriella ..."

"I thought we were going to *Singapore*." She picked up one of the silver knives, and then dropped it, as though surprised to find it in her hand.

"Gabriella," said Vishinski, with a calmness and a gravity that surprised him, "Shut up and listen to me. You lived in a post-communist society, just like I did. You know what it was like—gangsters, politicians, businessmen, military, all in it together, no real difference. Well, that's the way of the whole world now. The people behind this scheme are the richest and most powerful in the world, and the game they are playing is for immortality, and a way out of this stinking world before it craps out. If they even suspect that someone is talking about this scheme of theirs, that person will be swatted like a fly. You, me, anyone."

"Little boys' games," she said, but without much conviction. "Waving their ..."

"Gabriella," he said. "You remember Tod Twombly?"

"The software ... the billionaire guy ..."

"That's him. He was one of my clients and I made a lot of money off him. He wanted to kill me at one point. Anyway, we'll meet him on the island. His wife won't be there. He told her, which none of us was supposed to do. She told a friend, and she told ... well ... So they came to Twombly and they said, you have a choice. He could watch his wife being killed in front of him, and he could still go on the ship, or they would kill him straight away and her later. Obviously, he wanted to live, which is why he's there, and there was a spare place to be sold. Oh, and there were several traffic fatalities and one unexplained knife attack."

Gabriella sat silent for a while, a small tear running down one cheek. But she would get over it eventually. They had eternity, after all. On the whole, Vishinski thought, Gabriella was a good idea. She was Romanian, for a start, and had come to the U.S. without any money. If she had a family, she never spoke of them. She had also spent several years at university studying something, he forgot what, before starting a short career as a model and actress. She was just as keen on money as Amy had been, but at least it was for something Vishinski could understand—shopping—rather than for giving to deadbeats who claimed that destroying a piano with a pneumatic drill was a kind of art. Though it might be, actually, for all he knew about art. Meanwhile, Amy's lawyers would be discovering about now that the family assets—all in his name except for Amy's art collection—had been sold, and the money had disappeared. He wondered idly how she would pay their fees.

The flight deck door opened, and the copilot poked his head through.

"May I know, sir, whether you confirm that there is no date set for us to come and collect you?"

"That's right," said Vishinski. "Don't worry, we'll give the leasing company plenty of warning."

"Thank you, sir." The copilot disappeared. What he didn't know, of course, was that the plane (rented for a week at Gabriella's insistence, as the ultimate status symbol) had already had its lease canceled, and he was out of a job.

The 737 began its approach, and Sutcliffe stared out of the window at nothing in particular. They passed over a couple of boats casting off from a jetty; the last remnants of the crews who had rehabilitated the airfield, he supposed. Half a dozen aircraft were parked outside an improvised terminal, and the other 737, after discharging its passengers, was already preparing to leave.

They clambered out and down the steps, their luggage taken by a couple of brown-skinned men in neat white uniforms, who loaded it onto a trolley. The heat and humidity were paralyzing, but it was only a few steps into a massive marquee tent with some kind of air conditioning. There were bottles of champagne and canapés everywhere, and presiding over everything, Stahlman himself, with his beatific smile, leading his wife, a short, bejeweled, and obviously bewildered woman, behind him. There were the kind of stilted conversations underway between people who had nothing to say to each other, and could no longer use or exploit each other to make deals. A number of couples stood around awkwardly, looking as if one or both was going to panic, and clearly unable to comfort each other. A recently divorced gay couple of financiers, who had signed up for the trip long before, were conspicuously avoiding each other. Several small groups watched the aircraft taking off, with unreadable expressions on their faces. The last plane to leave carried the air movements team.

At 1300, after a bottle or so of champagne, Sutcliffe saw the little brown skinned men in neat white uniforms start to leave. They would take the last boat, back to wherever. He wondered idly if they would ever be paid.

When they were finally all alone, Stahlman called for silence, and stepped—hopped really—onto a little podium, looking down, and radiating enthusiasm and confidence.

"Welcome everyone, glad you could make it. Our friends will be here . . . ."

And suddenly between two heartbeats, there were twenty or more of the black figures, collecting up empty bottles, and starting to move the luggage.

"The ships will be landing in a few minutes," said every solid surface in the marquee. "Please remain where you are, since getting too close to the ships when they are landing can be dangerous, and for some time afterwards as well. We will load the baggage, and also take care of the final assessments of gold holdings."

One of the messengers raised a hand, and a screen full of data appeared in the air. Everyone crowded around, pushing, shoving and in some cases kicking each other to get a better view. Names scrolled down in order of gold owned.

"These are the final figures as at thirteen hundred local," said the chair next to Sutcliffe. "They take account of all transactions and gold purchases up to that point. You can see where you are in the list, and so what your status on the ship, and your status on our world, will be. Now please wait while the gold is loaded onto one of the ships."

A couple of the messengers pulled back one side of the marquee, and there they were: two ships, one about ten meters long, and one an order of magnitude larger, parked over the other side of the airfield. Or not parked precisely: something in their appearance suggested they were hovering a few millimeters above the ground. Both had the same black, watery sheen.

Meanwhile people were reading, with more or less pleasure, their positions off the slowly scrolling screen in the air. There were whoops of joy and cries of despair, complaints, and heated allegations of cheating. Several fights had already started. Stahlman, to nobody's surprise, came out on top, and a German politician came at the bottom of the list. Sutcliffe was about halfway up, not bad. De Kock had come in fifth, and was grinning massively, punching the air, and saying, "Ja, no, man, this is better than winning the Currie Cup!"

The gold was loaded quickly and efficiently by the messengers, who seemed to have almost supernatural strength, and carried boxes weighting tons between two of them. After that, they retreated, forming a line to stop people getting too close as the little shuttle took off again. But the departure was disappointing: the ship simply lifted, silently and quickly, as though an invisible giant hand had picked it up.

Sutcliffe looked reflexively at his watch, though he wasn't sure what time zone he was in. It must be time to board the ship now. Presumably someone would tell them. He looked up. There were no messengers. They must be outside. A little disturbed, he walked through the open side of the marquee, in the direction of the other ship. There was no ship. A trickle of people followed him.

There are some shocks that are so sudden and so total that they cannot actually be absorbed. Hundreds of wealthy people in expensive clothes goggled, open-eyed, at the absence of everything, and looked around for their people to explain it to them. There were no people. There was nothing except a completely empty airfield, and a marquee full of puzzled, frightened and slightly drunk rich people, with empty bottles of champagne and some dead canapés.

Hundreds of hands went to pockets and bags and took out mobile phones. Hundreds of heads tilted back in surprise.

"There's no signal," said a pony-tailed man standing next to Vishinski.

"Of *course* there's no signal," said Gabriella crushingly. "Have you any idea how far away the nearest telephone mast is?"

"But there's always a signal," mumbled the man, the billionaire owner of a tax-avoidance software company." The money I pay ... Anyway how would you know?

"I studied physics, once," said Gabriella, "and if there's one thing I know about, it's radio wave propagation."

"*On s'est faits enculés, quoi, tu sais ce que j'veux dire ?*" said a remarkably tall black man, the former dictator of a poor African state, famous for his calm good humor while watching his enemies being tortured to death. He had recently sold most of his property portfolio, itself funded by the looting of the last of his country's mineral assets, to buy gold, including some he had earlier sold to buy property.

"*T'as raison, mec. Ils se foutent de nos gueules, et comment !*" agreed his neighbor, a Lebanese businessman who had been his financial advisor.

"Look," said somebody gesticulating wildly, almost sobbing. The runway was slowly disappearing, dust and debris flying into the air, as though some invisible monster was jumping up and down repeatedly with heavy boots. In a minute or so there was no runway, only piles of rubble.

From the back of the crowd there came a scream of anger and despair as one of the disappointed investors hurled his phone to the ground and began to stamp on it, chanting obscenities in Russian. He burst out into actual tears, and his cry was taken up by those around him, running through the crowd like a spreading stain, and turning into the uncomprehending cry of a wounded animal.

"You are criminal," said a Korean telecoms billionaire standing next to Stahlman. "You take my money and buy gold and you give me nothing. You are criminal."

"Now look," said Stahlman, recovering his composure a little, and striving for his Congressional-appearance persona. "It's clear that some things have not gone quite as planned …"

"You are criminal," repeated the Korean calmly. "You will suffer."

"Bastard," cried a small voice. It was a Thai woman, who, through a series of husbands, had controlled the trade in the last few endangered species in the region for thirty years. "Bastard, I gave you all my money." She pushed Stahlman violently with her Gucci umbrella, and he was so surprised he actually fell over. He lay on the ground, winded certainly, but more importantly just unable to grasp what was happening, the victim of a hostile act for probably the first time in his life.

The woman looked around and grabbed the first thing she saw, an empty champagne bottle. She brought it down on Stahlman's head as he started to get to his feet. He fell back, blood running from his nose. She hit him again. And again.

From behind them, the moan of the crowd modulated gradually into a roar of anger, and those at the back pushed those in the front forward, trampling some underfoot. Before Stahlman could move, he and the Thai woman disappeared under a scrum of bodies, hacking and kicking at Stahlman's prostrate form.

"You cretin!" said Gabriella looking at Vishinski as if she wanted to murder him. "Didn't it occur to you to actually fucking check, I mean, didn't you think of looking it up in, for example, Wikipedia or something, looking to see if gold was actually as rare as they told you? Don't you even have a *brain*?"

"I …" began Vishinski helplessly, but stopped as he heard shouting from a group who were standing outside the marquee, looking out to sea. "What are they … they're saying there's a *ship*."

There was a ship, several hundred meters away, the ship which was taking the small brown people in white uniforms away, but for some reason had yet to cast off from a long wooden pier.

"Ja ……" the beefy South African took off like a rocket, followed, a few moments later, by dozens of others, the women tripping and falling in their high heels. Even the crowd who were kicking Stahlman to death stopped what they were doing for a moment, and looked up.

The South African crashed through a line of women who were hobbling with difficulty towards the cliff, and reached the end of the bridge, puffing and starting to stagger a bit. The ship was just casting off, and the South African waved his arms furiously, screaming, "Stop!"

But all of a sudden the pier started to vanish, tiny fragments flying into the air and settling onto the water like rain. The pier lurched downwards, catapulting the South African into the sea, before evaporating entirely a few seconds later as though eaten by an invisible, supersonic swarm of termites. The fastest pursuers onto the bridge were caught by whatever terrible power the aliens were wielding. A second or two later, all that was visible was a brown scum on the surface of the water, with occasional patches of red.

"Help me," came the scream from far below. Whatever De Kock's skills as a rugby player, he was obviously no swimmer, and he was already floundering in his safari gear and heavy boots. In fact, there was nothing they could do, even had anyone been interested. The cliff was ten meters high and effectively sheer. He was trying desperately to climb up, but there was nothing to hold on to. After a while, people started to wander away, and there were only a few left watching him when he drowned.

Sutcliffe sat in the shadow of a rock, the broken champagne bottle by his right hand. He had no regrets about what he was going to do.

Thinking about it, his life had always been pretty much shit, and he'd wanted to end it somehow for about as long as he could remember. The only times he had ever been happy had been when he was triumphing over others, and even that had grown repetitive and boring with the passage of time. He'd been killing himself slowly with alcohol and drugs because he had never had the courage to kill himself quickly with something else.

And he was going to die anyway. Exhausted, dehydrated, sun-struck and starving, the group was slowly perishing. Dead and dying bodies were everywhere. Two days had passed, and Sutcliffe was bleakly aware that no one would come to save them now. They had, after all, covered their tracks well. It would be weeks, if not longer, before anyone even wondered where they were, and whether to start looking. He had seen people get murdered in an access of hysteria, throw themselves off cliffs in despair, and just keel over from stress and exhaustion. One woman had died choking, trying to dry-swallow a handful of heart tablets. Better to get it over with.

Picking up a shard of glass, he made the first cut.

The light display on the vessel that was not really a vessel at all, and had no name because it did not need one, showed the little shuttle-construct returning, entering through an iris of light that closed seamlessly behind it.

From behind came the tones of *Politeness-to-Superior/Entry/Query/Welcome?*

Politeness-to-Inferior/Entry/Pleasure, sent the First, turning away from the display, which had now gone back to showing the usual star-field.

"If you are interested," said the Second, "we have a scrying image now from over the island. I can generalize it."

"What does it show? What we expected?"

"Worse, actually. Half of them seem to be killing the other half."

There was a silence. *Relief/Conclusion/Sadness/Mutual*

"We thought it was going to be, well, bad."

"It was the whole point of the exercise, if you remember. Get the greediest and most ruthless specimens of humanity to select themselves, to maroon themselves somewhere, and then let them die. I admit ... well, we didn't quite expect they'd be killing each other, as well. Or at least not so enthusiastically."

Spirit/Obedience/Higher-Understanding

"Yes, all deindustrialization is difficult, even with the help of the Spirit." *Obeisance*. "We can only do so much to help. Here and there we have succeeded and elsewhere we've failed. If this planet is to have any chance of a way out, people like that have to be got rid of. Not all humans are like that, you know. We've watched them for long enough, we've seen how many of them are trying to adapt, trying to survive."

"Don't forget this is a planet which uses money. Every planet that uses money risks destroying itself."

"And?"

"Well, a lot of these people weren't involved with money, in the sense that we've seen elsewhere. They had already bought and sold everything that was tradable. Then they started trading things that didn't actually exist, but might. They were *buying and selling money*, if you can imagine such a thing. And in the end they were selling money to buy gold. They were turning everything into gold. We took all the main players in this mad game away at one go, or most of them anyway. It looks like things they call "banks," that gamble with money, are closing down in a lot of countries. Their whole economic system is crashing, and with a bit of luck, there won't be anybody to replace these idiots."

"And that's all good?"

"Objectively, perhaps, no. But if you think of the alternatives ... This is their best shot at peaceful deindustrialization, frankly. Probably their only one."

Politeness/Pause/Reflection
Politeness/Pause/Mutual

"What shall we do with the gold?"

"Put it through the Transmuter, turn it into something useful."

They both stared at the light display, which had now changed to show Saturn and its rings, a sight which the First thought he could probably keep looking at forever.

It's a liquid, thought Vishinski. If I can drink it, it may keep me alive a bit longer. He wondered if he had the strength, though. Held gingerly in his hand was the sharpest piece of glass he had been able to find. He wished he knew a bit more about survival. He wished he knew a bit more about anything; that any of them had known anything about anything, other than moving numbers around to make them look bigger. His grandfather, he thought vaguely, would have known what to do. He had fought in the Great Patriotic War, and been a reserve officer in the Engineers for a long time. If there was a way out, his grandfather would have found it. Or maybe Tariq would have found it. But Tariq was a multi-millionaire now, running a medical insurance arbitrage company.

But no point thinking about that now. He had no choice: he was so weak that it would be all he could do to reach the nearest corpse. Very slowly, he began to roll over. He had no idea whose body it was. Gabriella had a blue dress like that but it could be somebody else as well. In the blinding sun he could not be sure. He reached the body after about ten minutes, panting and dizzy with fatigue and dehydration. Where to cut? Where would the blood come out most easily? Would he actually be able to drink it? Where was the shard of glass? It had been there a minute ago. He decided to rest for a moment. And a moment more. And eventually, he lay unmoving, a trickle of blood seeping from the wound in his hand, eyes open, staring at the unfeeling sky, as though seeking something.

Eric Rust Backos

True Math

Eyes that were not human watched as a slight, fair-skinned high school girl piloted an old white four-door pickup around potholes and puddles south on Leaf Street in Edwardtown, Maple County, Ohio. Unruly dark red hair stuck out from under a white golf cap, its logo obscured by freebie sunglasses resting on the visor, unneeded on a rainy autumn afternoon. The many eyes blinked and moved around fearfully, the collective behind them disturbed by the noise and movement of the vehicle.

Then the truck passed, and the sparrows returned to feeding on the abundant gifts of a long, cool summer.

ON THE SATURDAY of Labor Day weekend, Hans Rietveld's tidy, gray Tacoma was parked on Leaf Street in front of Rikki's house, or, more accurately, his late grandparents' house. "Rikki Rush" and "my boyfriend" still sounded odd together, but I liked it. His mom lived in the married-faculty apartment building on the Holder campus. Good for me while Mom and I lived in an apartment across the street from Holder until the farmhouse was remodeled. It was looking pretty foregone that Rikki was going to take over this house, a narrow Craftsman-style, built for a railroad worker back when the city and railroads were important. The tracks and a lumpy grade crossing were only three doors down.

What do you do when you find an entire railroad just lying on the ground forgotten?

Moving from the hood in Akron to Edwardtown when Mom and I inherited a tumbledown farm was quite a shock. Pile on a crazy rural-urban mix in the high school; a shrine for Erielhonan, the Lady of Lake Erie, in my side yard; and the discovery that *Star's Reach*, the quirky and long-running TV science fiction/fantasy/adventure show, is filled with useful, factual information about the world. All that should be enough to turn anyone into a nervous wreck, right?

Fortunately, a blind date with an Edwardtown High School rugby player named Rikki Rush put all that in perspective. Having a best-friend-in-law like Hans Rietveld really helps too. These guys actually do things and make things. They're nothing like the sports fans I slung pitchers and cheese fries to in the undergrounds.

Rikki pulls reality into existence.

While that thought rolled around in my head, I parked my Travelette in the driveway and slid off the seat onto the broken concrete and into the rain. My boots found a puddle on the first try. I opened the gate into the backyard where Rikki's worn, probably red Power Wagon sat in front of a detached garage twice as big as the house, walked around to the kitchen entrance, and let myself in.

Hans had his back to the door and Rikki faced me as I opened the storm door and stepped inside. The house was warmer than the outside, but still cold.

Rikki looked up from the kitchen table, smiled, and said, "Hiya, Bellavee!" He was tall, at least when he stood up, and had tannish skin that revealed the strangely mixed ancestry typical in Ohio's Western Reserve, brownish hair, and green eyes. Rikki was usually busy on some project or another with Hans except when he was doing "Druid stuff": working on ordination in a religion that was popular here but unheard of in Akron.

Hans was a Green Wizard, a member of the eponymous engineering group and farm co-op that embraced low-tech solutions. He was also a third-generation resident of Little Capetown where expat Afrikaans speakers from all over the Dark Continent settled without regard to their looks or ancestries. A common language held the neighborhood together even though its origin was the entire southern half of Africa. Hans, however, looked Afrikaner: shiny black hair, bright blue eyes, and fair skin made him generically "white" in contrast with Rikki's question mark in the space labeled "race."

I have friends.

Hans did not look up and said, "Bellavee Merrymount-Morton, how are you?" and continued writing something on a scratch pad.

The boys were huddled over what looked like math homework, which had become much more interesting since I moved here from Akron because EHS followed the broader trend of dumping calculators and computers for slide rules. Calculators were relegated to an optional, no-credit class for the shrinking number of college-bound graduating seniors.

Hans was still writing as I walked across the kitchen and leaned on Rikki. He leaned back on me like a giant cat.

Eventually, I grabbed an old wool blanket from the back of the couch, wrapped it around my shoulders, pulled up a chair, and sat leaning on my boyfriend. The tag on the blanket read,

Orrlaskan
The Orr Felt & Blanket Co.
in Piqua, Ohio, USA

The words framed a picture of a man driving, wait, mushing a dog sled.

Rikki saw me looking at the tag and asked, "Did you see the bit in the *Telegram* about businesses killed by globalization coming back now that shipping has gotten so expensive? Orr got mentioned."

I gave my best fake horror expression, "You mean using *technology* so container ships can play dodge-'em cars with icebergs doesn't work?"

Hans imitated an aging chemistry teacher who really believed in The Future!™. "Nooo! It must work! Man is the Conqueror of the Stars!"

We laughed. The boys went back to their project.

There was a polar projection drawn on posterboard on the table, but I didn't recognize many of the symbols labeling various features. A grab-bag of small silver and copper coins were laid out on it, most marked in languages I didn't recognize, the result looking much like a complicated checkers game as the boys moved, stacked, and removed coins.

Rikki was holding a nice slide rule like the ones Jim's Radios sold, but the markings were, well, they must have been for some very advanced math. It was yellowish-white like old piano keys and covered with symbols I'd never seen as well as regular numbers and letters.

The boys paused to look at their results, so I asked, "May I see your slipstick?"

Rikki handed it to me. It was light for its size, about a foot long and four inches wide. At the top edge, dark wood showed between the outer layers of white material. I could read Anchester Slide Rules, Ltd, UK on the worn leather case in front of him, but Exham Calc. Inst. / No. 3363 / England was stamped on the gold-colored metal brace that held the frame together.

Wait, is that orichalcum?

"Is this real ivory?" I asked as I moved the slide back and forth. It was tight in the frame, slid smoothly, and stayed put after a calculation. It was, in other words, nothing like the battered plastic or cardstock slide rules Edwardtown High School used.

Rikki said, "Maybe," and pushed a shirt-pocket-size manual with a heavy green fabric cover over to me. I picked it up while the boys were calculating.

The copyright was 1980. "The Exham Alchemical Slide Rule, Number 3363, is a ten-inch duplex model made of mahogany* and ivory** with eight scales on each side." The asterisks directed me to an extraordinarily British apology in the lower margin. "Due to supply shortages, the wood may or may not be mahogany, and the ivory might be new or salvaged material from elephants or walruses, or it might be made from treated bone, wood or tagua nuts."

Then the manual got weird. It said, "Using symbolic logic calculation as part of the cognitive-meditative process of magic helps improve outcomes by requiring a well-defined goal and providing a clear path to it in the form of a topological map of 8-dimensional Lobachevskian hyperspace, in which every point in the eight dimensions is in direct contact with every other point."

"What," I demanded, pointing at the paragraph, "does that mean?"

Hans used one of the coins on the graph for a monocle and skewered the *teddibly Britash* manual with a pretentious upper-crust accent, "As we say in Dreary Old England, understand the topology and, *Blip!* there you are, pip-pip, cheerio, wot?" He pretended to open a brolly and check a pocket watch.

Rikki rolled his eyes.

"Seriously," I glared at Hans, "Does this say the math helps me think magic into reality?"

The boys stopped what they were doing, looked at each other, looked at me, and then Rikki said, "A-yalp," with the Yankee tongue click on the end.

Then Hans pushed over a pamphlet that looked like the Maple County standard paper cup with a white background, green stripe, and repeating daisy-bammut-daisy motif. Now that I had seen bits of green Hyperborean pottery left behind by the last ice age, I knew where the daisy and miniature woolly mammoth motif originated. How Manly Wade Wellman's moniker for padded pachyderms stuck to Ohio's big brown cryptid, nobody seemed to know.

I know about them. They aren't cryptids any more.

I saw the title: *Die Handboek van die Okkulte Skuifliniaal*, Geskryf deur Kraals Notch, Hoofstuk Veertien. I picked it up and found it filled with tables full of numbers, letters from several languages, and sets of symbols that didn't seem to have much to do with each other. Diagrams of slide rules and sample calculations showed how to use the strange markings.

All the Afrikaans I knew covered two subjects, food and rugby. I guessed at "handbook," *skrif* must be "script," written, and v sounds like f, fourteen?

Occult slide rule?

The boys were laying out the coins again, so I picked up the slipstick and pushed the slide and the cursor back and forth to match a string of drawings in the pamphlet. The rule seemed to hum and warm up in a happy way. When Rikki finished with the coins, I passed the rule back to him. The rule's reaction would have sent me running only a few months ago. Now? Not surprising. Not surprising that I liked it, either.

I considered the interesting contents of Rikki's garage and asked, "Did the slide rule come with the workshop?"

The boys chuckled, and Rikki said, "No, in seventh grade, the class troublemaker, Anders Bohrman, heard me say I liked slide rules, so he offered to sell me his dad's old one. Somehow, we negotiated fourteen dollars as a fair price, but I didn't have it and asked my mom. She figured something was wrong with Anders' offer and wrote a check. Anders tried to sign it over to his dealer for some meth, that kid did the same with a real dealer, and when the check hit the bank, all three were arrested."

"Meth, the no-wonder drug." I knew its scourge from Akron, though I'd yet to see it here.

Hans looked pained. "Right. It gets worse."

Rikki continued, "Anders' dad called my mom and asked what I was doing with the rule, a family hand-me-down that nobody really wanted. Fortunately for me, I was sitting at the kitchen table working on the first problem in the manual, so he said if I'm that interested, I can keep it."

Hans picked up, "The dealer went to prison, the other kid got juvie, and Anders' dad sent him to boot camp where he fell off a cliff, possibly with some help, though that was never proven."

Rikki finished, "Hans saw it on my bookshelf, told Oupa Freeman, and they've been training me on the sly. Keep that between us. Not everybody loves these things, and others want them."

Hans nodded in agreement.

He moved the slide and looked at the result.

Hans asked, "What did you get?"

"Two ankh alpha at two falcons when I divide by iron before the river."

Hans moved a couple of coins around.

"You aren't doing math, exactly," I observed.

Hans said, "Um. I guess you should tell her."

"Um." Rikki said a little sheepishly, "I wanted to surprise you, but no dice. We're following the flow of voor to try and find your bowl."

Voor. The life force.

Something like awe and a bit like fear rose inside me.

"Erielhonan's bowl," I corrected, and imagined it as I'd seen it in my dreams: blood-red mineral water from the artesian well up the hill filling a stone bowl and flowing back out clear and sparkling blue in bright sunshine.

Hans asked, "We're talking about bammuts. What do you get when you flip the slide to bridge the river and divide by Elephant?"

"A headache. Water leopard. Again."

"Water leopard?" I asked.

"Lake otter," they said at the same time. The formerly extinct two-hundred-pound comeback kid and Holder College mascot who lived in the Great Lakes and their tributaries.

"Might be leopard in the water, but you get the idea," Rikki explained, pointing at a string of strange symbols on his scratch pad.

I give up. I'll ask.

"So … what are you calculating?" I hated admitting cluelessness.

Hans was running his finger down a table in Notch, "Tells you how strong voor fields are using Prynne coefficients. That's how we're plotting where your, er, Erielhonan's bowl might be. The voor flows around like weather fronts, and the calculations help draw the TV weather map patterns you see with the coins. Other stuff, too."

Nope. Still don't know. Wait … English Class.

"Prynne?" I asked cautiously.

Hans said, "What, you thought *The Crucible* was about McCarthyism?"

I growled, "Quit yanking my chain. Hester Prynne's in *The Scarlet Letter*."

"Okay," Hans agreed, "the real one wrote a pile of books on math and …" He waved his hand at the contents of the table.

I felt a little sarcasm coming on and said, "And Elizabeth Proctor was no slouch, I suppose."

The boys looked at each other and laughed, then Hans looked at me with respect and said, "No, she was not."

Rikki added, "You see how we search for True History in the rubble."

Wait. He's serious!

"I found a 'clew,' a ball of string to follow, like your uncle the lit teacher says?" I sounded surprised.

So, this is what you do when you find an entire railroad just lying on the ground forgotten.

Rikki said, "A-yalp," with the tongue click, and made another note.

"Okay." I waved at the things on the table. "Why did this get so mistreated in the middle of the twentieth century?"

Rikki shrugged. "My mom teaches lit, and she says the writers were trying to make a cold, dead universe where everything's free for the taking."

That explains the whole twentieth century.

"All of which gets me?" I was starting to see sense.

Rikki pointed to a diagram in Notch, "You can plot out this swirl pattern to find lost things. You see the problem in the coins; a bunch of swirls and no center. We need bammuts and lake otters in the same place."

"There's a lake otter in Bowl Creek behind my house, and we know that a bammut visits the shrine," I volunteered, "can you work backwards from the farm?"

The boys looked at each other, Hans grabbed an old road atlas out of his backpack on the floor, and Rikki scribbled a new center onto his scratch pad.

Well?

"Well?" asked Hans.

Rikki flipped the slide over. I saw his ears twitch from my spot behind his left shoulder.

"Elephant and water leopard," he said.

They were getting excited,

Rikki checked his notes, then pushed the slide back and forth twice, scribbling each time. Then he turned it so Hans could read his marks.

"Stone, hill, blossom, tree, rice paddy, anth and ulth are both empty jar," then Hans moved the coins around until they stood in a neat stack at the center of the polar-like graph.

I asked, "Does that mean 'Cobble Knoll Apple Orchard' and here?"

Hans imitated Rikki's deadpan, "Ah-yalp," with the Yankee tongue click.

But I'd gotten skunked too many times already trying to find Erielhonan's bowl.

"We're looking for a bread bowl on a five-hundred-acre farm," I pouted.

"Your farm," Hans pronounced, "Check your cards."

"Okay," and I pulled out my Gypsy Witch cards.

"Where," I asked them, "should I look for Erielhonan's bowl on my farm?"

The House.

"Could you be specific?"

The Eye, the Moon, and for the third card, I fumbled and the Pig and the Flames fell in front of me. The Witch would use the pictures on her cards as well as the text to talk with me, and sometimes she would even use the playing card numbers and values. Paying attention and interpreting was my job.

I puzzled, "Look in the dark by the pig ... no the hog trough plus flames. Look in the basement by the hot water tank? But the basement is all mushroom farm. It'll be moved out when the new barn is finished."

Rikki observed, "No hot water tank? That makes no sense. Do you have a washer and dryer? Are they near the furnace?"

"Yeah, big commercial ones. Hey, I didn't see a water inlet either when I was down there."

"Boarded up, maybe. The occupants were stoners. Maybe there's a hidden access," Rikki offered.

"So, I'm supposed to find a secret panel with a sledge hammer?"

They stereoed, "Tape measure."

"What?"

Rikki continued, "That's how we find rooms and closets that have been dry-walled over and forgotten when we work for my grandfather. Measure and draw a floorplan until lost space shows up."

I blinked and remembered something important. "You don't have to draw. The blueprints are in the office trailer."

A thunderclap announced the arrival of the main part of the ongoing rainstorm from the west. A line of booms followed, each closer than the next. Then the lights went out. Rikki stood up, walked to the utility closet by the back door, and pulled the main breaker for the house.

Hans said, "Gonna hook up the generator?"

"Only if it gets cold. We can cook in the fireplace, if you like," Rikki offered while pulling out little brass candle-holding lanterns from the pantry.

Hans' walkie-talkie crackled. He answered, then said, "Gotta go. At least I drove this time."

Rikki grabbed his own much plainer radio and gave Hans a radio check, just in case. CB radios took some getting used to, but Maple County north of Two Turtles Hill has a shortage of cell towers, never mind a wobbly dollar putting cell phones out of reach.

We said our goodbyes, paused to catch up on some gossip, including efforts by Violet, the same friend who connected me with Rikki, to find Hans a Cider-Fest Dance date. Then we said goodbye again, and finally, Hans headed home to Edwardtown's last holdout nice neighborhood.

Walking distance, dark side of the Moon, whatever.

I could say the same about my farm, Cobble Knoll, only a few minutes down the highway and a few miles on a dirt road that would be impassable after this rainstorm until the road department grader arrived.

A few minutes later, Hans radioed to let us know he was home, then Rikki and I both called to check in with our moms. Shortly after that, more thunderclaps and wind announced another sideways deluge. Rikki threw a match into an already laid pile of tinder and kindling in the blocky, angular hearth. The old house was small and neglected, but it had nice details.

"Look, a crane," he said proudly and swung a steel arm back and forth from the hearthstones to the fire. "I'm going to make a dozen or so of these and sell them at the Cider-Fest in October." Once the fire was going, he hung an old cast iron pot with

KAMP KETTLE KO.
EDWARDTOWN, O.

on the lid from the crane.

"Kamp Kettle Kompany?" I puzzled.

Rikki laughed, "The Camps were conductors on the Underground Railroad from Akron to here, then on to Erie. After the war, they were Anti-Poke Noses, sworn to oppose the Klan. Humor was one of their better weapons. Seems everybody but the Klansmen were in on it, and they just loved filling their kitchens with Kamp Kast Kollections. Too bad the business didn't survive the arrival of stainless steel."

I thought about the transportation problems in the news and wondered if the Camp foundry might have a market again.

"Maybe," I suggested, "you could call your project the Camp Crane Company?"

A little while later, we ate homemade soup from big mugs while sitting on the couch, Rikki on the left end, me curled on his right.

After that, we drank tea and lounged in front of the fire. The thunder passed on to the east, and the rain changed from horizontal to a steady vertical patter. Rikki turned on an old boombox, antenna extended with a wire coat hanger, and tuned in Holder's student-run station. At the bottom of the hour, the DJ dutifully reported yet another round of broken storm drains and gas pipes under the crumbling brick streets that blocked the easy routes to my farm.

Rikki intoned, "You can't get there from here."

I saw his point, so I curled up next to him and put my head on his shoulder.

You can't get there from here, but I like it here.

G. Kay Bishop

Kedorra's Kin

IN THE ANCIENT DAYS, when Ashtameht was young and the womb-borne Three were even yet wordless babes, then it was accustomed for the eldest woman of the hearth to be the merciful giver of death. It was crones' wisdom that taught her to root up the easeful lily, prepare the buttercup wine, or mix the asphodel and honeyed hemlock, the sweet and the sleep together.

How eagerly did men then suckle the wooden nipple! Men battle-torn beyond healing, men with the gangrene—these smiled upon the wrinkled hands that opened the locked Gate of the Places Beyond. How gratefully did women sip from the golden gourd: women eaten within and without by the white tumors—women whose bellies rotted within yet died not.

The world then was sore beset by countless Rings of Power: places of swift evil and early death; of slow-strickening and long sorrows wherein sores, bruising, blood sacs weighing on the lungs, blackened teeth were visited upon young and old alike. Mothers failed of fruitful birthing as horrors of clotted flesh dropped untimely to earth, and no child born there ever thrived.

These Rings of Powers un-Known and Nameless were many and of many kinds. For some, the land seemed good and ran with abundant game, yet the peoples who dwelt there diminished soon and died. Others yielded only stunted and deformed crops and the peoples thereof died of starvation.

Then it was that the ones we call witches began to be born among us: gut witches, dairy witches, beer witches, and all others who have a special Knowledge of the Little Ones. Their auguries and sensings warn us of places to avoid. Likewise, the Men of the Soil who can smell metals, taste and spit out sourness, overripe molds and other bad soils that harm the folk who eat of such taint. Without these, none could have remained. The Rings of Power brought such evil that the world was all but unpeopled, and all the Labors of Ashtameht seemed like to be in vain.

Not until the Great Tumult in which the Third Daughter was born of the mouth and not the belly — the Hour in which Ashtameht cast up from her vitals the Poison she had been given — aye! when She vomited out the vileness which her Son's lust mixed with the Waters of Truth — only then were these many Rings broken and the demons thereof destroyed by the Third Daughter.

Not until the whole world was deep-double digged, as mountains folded and rivers of red rock ran free and the Stars in their former courses were vastly Changed did the sore need of easeful death from the Sacred Cup lessen.

Fewer now than in those times are folk who have such need. Fewer still are those who dare to speak or act a discourteous thing, willful in offense against the queen of their hearth, their old yedame. For if too often defied, too grossly dishonored, she kept still this one power, if she live so long: to withhold the final gift at her own will — and who could say whether or no they would have need of it at the last?

Yet sorrowful nonetheless are these latter days, when the carven cup is too often proffered to young husbands burnt like roasted pigs when the cruel enmity of the Sun Warriors sets fire to the ripened grain and drives the reapers into the flames, spitted upon iron-pointed spears.

Alas! that old hands now minister to mothers bereft of children and husbands all at the hands of ceaseless, causeless hate. How defiantly do the proud maidens drink! They who will not to become slaves, nor bear the spawn of brutes, nor endure the beatings, nor suffer long the shame of subjugation. 'Tis the old yedames who weep, and themselves taste their own medicine, after all their kin have drunk.

The tale is told of one maiden, Kedorra by name, of the Hearth Dondimagia. Long had that family abided in that place. The vines of that House were mightier than strong men's thews, famous and rightly so, for they had been husbanded many generations. The men of Dondimagia wore skirts of purple and tabards of velvet, and their feet were shod in fine leather. The women went in cloth of silver and clustered rubies did they wear. Proud were the Dondimagia, yet wise and courteous withal. Folk far and away gave them a good name. The yedame of the house was very old and when this story begins, she ailed a good deal.

It was the custom then that when the yedames grew weary of their own lives, they should teach the crones' mysteries to one of the household, old and wise, before they departed this Realm.

The one they chose would then be the queen of the hearth, acknowledged by all as the true head of the household, and the arbiter of every hard judgment.

All women strove to be worthy of that honor, and whenever the festivals were held for harvest or fruiting, plowing or planting, while the men assayed their strength in bouts of wrestling or threshing contests, then did the women hold games of judgment and set each other to guessing riddles. For it would be the wisest who was made yedame in place of the eldest. Thus did they improve in wisdom by practice and much thinking on matters of weight.

Only Kedorra did not take part in these games, though she too was a sister of the House. Kedorra was the youngest of all and, indeed, she killed her mother in coming into this world. It was thought to be an ill omen, for her mother had been much beloved, and the child was ill-favored besides. Yet in that household there was honor, and she was not carried out to be exposed on the stony hillside as Manimonean law decreed for girls born deformed.

Instead the yedame Ameilia nurtured her and raised her up to be her own, and when Kedorra was fifteen she gladly returned the care; for it was she who tended to the old woman, and was like to her shadow. She too was bent over, though not with age.

Kedorra was so plain of face and so twisted of body that none would ever think to mate with her. Her sisters pitied her but troubled themselves not about her overmuch. Had she not a place of her own? And indeed, Kedorra was content and strove not for marks of anyone's favor, neither dainty food nor fine raiment, nor any other good thing. She accepted all that was given her, even the cast-off clothing of the serving maid, and made no murmur. For in that house, the serving maids were clad well enough for any of us ordinary folk!

Yedame Ameilia departed from this Realm when Kedorra was eighteen years of age, To the deformed girl, she confided the secrets that were best poured into older and wiser ears. But she was old and tired and foresaw that to choose just one of the proud sisters would be to sow discord in a household where there had been none for many long years. So she taught her caretaker how to give the last rites and walked away out of her pain, going northward, into the woods. But Kedorra said nothing to the rest of her family, accepting this gift as she had all the others, even the gift of her own life.

Time passed and troubles came. The countryfolk on every side were embroiled in wars and skirmishes. Though the House of Dondimagia was never approached by enemies, yet enemies came closer every season, and friends were fewer. Finally, there came a day when the ruin of all they had loved and known was plainly in sight. The family gathered to judge what course of action they must take in this extremity.

"Alas! What shall we do! For our yedame is gone and she named not her successor! Now we see the reason for her neglect. Surely she foresaw this evil day and knew that the House of Dondi and Magia was destined for this bitter end!"

Then it was that Kedorra revealed to her family that she had been anointed by Ameilia. And they all marvelled at this. But Kedorra showed her wisdom, saying to them, "Let all who will depart from this place. Let us live abroad, free from the oppressors' deathly hands, unyoked and driven not by the whip, yet in exile, far from the land of our mothers."

But the proud sisters wept and their husbands rent their garments and all cried out against this saying. To leave the place of their long mothers before them was worse than death! And yet how could they endure to see this beloved place ruled by hated masters, overlords with whips and chains to force them to labor or send them into exile unwilling!

On their knees they cast themselves before her and begged for an easy death. For they knew the cruelty of those who came against them, and the strength of their numbers. Then again did Kedorra counsel them, speaking gently and bidding them put sorrow aside for one day only.

"Let us prepare a feast, to eat, drink, and be merry, for tomorrow, who knows what it will bring?"

And they dried their tears and did as she bade them, willingly, cheerfully; even as she had accepted their leavings, so now did they accept her guidance in this their sorest hour of trial. All was done as she bade them, even to the songs she favored most to hear. What joy and kindness, what music and dancing, feasting and making love! Never was there such a frolic as that of Kedorra's kin in the eleventh hour of their ruling days.

The merrymaking went on long into the evening, and all retired to their beds, confident in the counsel of the yedame Kedorra, to take whatever might come upon the morrow.

When the armies marched over Dondimagian lands, they came in seeming courtesy, taking good care to follow the roads. They trampled not the fields, nor burned the barns, for the fields were famed, and the vineyards much prized.

Kedorra answered the door, as if she were the serving maid, and bade all the captains enter, with the same respect as if they had come on an honest errand.

The commander-general announced his name—it was not recorded in the Book the last time I looked, so I cannot tell it to you—and desired that his presence be made known to the family.

"All are abed, good sir," she replied mildly, "for we had much feasting here yesternight, and none of the family has yet risen. Wouldst care to wait a while? There is refreshment at hand." She indicated the casks and bottles that stood all about the house.

He and all his captains chose sealed vessels—they were not such fools as to accept drink from a vessel that had been standing open overnight! Each man's choice was better than the next and they spent some time comparing the various excellencies of the wines. The commander-general, growing somewhat impatient, soon inquired after the head of the family.

Kedorra replied, "Yedame Ameilia departed, travelling northward, into the woods, some two years ago. She has not yet returned."

The man frowned.

"I *meant* to ask after the *man* who is head of the family."

"I know not who that might be, good sir, unless it be yourself. Here we have no customs save our own."

The commander-general then thought that this maid-servant had not the wit to know that he was come to seize this land and hold it for his king. Though he smiled at such folly, yet he was disgusted by her ill looks and would have her go.

"Very well, since I am now the head of the household, give my men to drink just as you have done for your own people. See to it."

"My pleasure, good sir," Kedorra answered and she departed to serve according to his will as she had always done with her sisters and their husbands. Once outside, she laboriously mounted the steps of the porch to be above the mounted men and said loudly, "The new head of this household bids you all welcome, and says that you are free to drink from any vessel you choose, be it butt, bottle, cask or barrel."

The men cheered, and laughed, for they had heard much praise of the stores of this house. They lost no time rolling out the best they could find and setting to with the best will in all the world. Only one captain refrained, and bade his men do likewise, for he thought it might be a trick of the enemy, to make all the men drunk and thus escape with whatever there might be of value in the house. He drank nothing himself, not even well water, save what he had with him from the last camp; but he could not restrain his men so far as to imitate him.

Nevertheless, they did drink more sparingly than the rest, for they were obedient in spite of their fellows' riotous ways. This captain told off his men to set a watch on the house.

No trap was laid for them, or none that he could tell. Not a soul stirred within, or without. There was only the deformed servant, and the troops kept her mightily busy, hustling about on her short, twisted legs, bringing out every vessel in the house—exquisite porcelain pottery, all of it—cups and carafes, bowls of all sizes, stout goblets of carven stone and chalices of swirling colored glass.

Even the cooking vessels she delivered up to them, for they were so very many—far more than that house had ever entertained before. In the spirit of the feasting, and of her own blessed life, Kedorra gave with open hand to all who asked.

Morning passed, slowly. High noon shone down upon the sleeping vineyards and upon the figures of many men at arms. Horses grazed at their ease, evening fell, and still the spell of slumber held motionless both the bodies of the House of Dondimagia and those of their conquerors. And they sleep there still, you know, for those who take their drink from the hands of the yedame, must accept whatever comes after.

The captain who drank nothing kept watch all alone for a while, until day's dusk fell and heart's understanding dawned upon him at the same time. Then he sprang to his feet and ran to the house, fearing, hoping and knowing not what he would do, yet something he must do or burst of sheer fright and heartache!

His fears were fully answered, though his hopes were dashed, even as all the bottles, glasses and fine chalices were dashed and broken into many shards. From room to room he passed, finding none alive, not one! The householders of Dondimagia lay as still in their beds (lovingly twined in one another's arms) as did the troops and all their officers; though the latter seemingly died alone (and in agony, not in peace, if their looks and their vomit could be taken as any measure), none touching any of his fellows in his final hour.

At last in the kitchen he came upon Kedorra. Her back was to him as he rushed in.

"Treachery!" he cried and drew his sword to slay her.

She turned then, and he beheld her deadly eyes, deeply shadowed in the gloaming, her club-fingered hands clumsily grasping the last, the loveliest, carven chalice he had ever seen.

"Yea, and theft beside, old man! Put up thy sword! My chalice is older by far than thy blade. Will you not accept the courtesy of this ancient house, and drink with me? Here, see—I do take the first sip as courtesy doth demand."

He saw her drink from the cup and then she offered it to him, slowly reaching towards him with her hideously blotched, inhuman, outstretched arms. The cup expanded twice, three times its normal size. It filled all his line of sight.

Almost he began to long for it, to wonder how it would taste—how good it would be to be free of his old, tired body. But he was a young man still, not yet forty years of age.

Realizing what he was thinking, he trembled with such uncontrollable fright that the sword dropped from his suddenly nerveless hand. She laughed.

> "What? Didst think that thou and thine
> Could cheaply come and buy the wine
>   Of the House of Dondimagia?
> Far more dear and far more fine
>   Is the drink of Dondimagia!
> Neither hot spilt blood nor the cold cast iron
>   Naught shalt thou have for thy pains!
> Nor gold nor grain nor slaves in chains
>   Wilt thou get at Dondimagia!
> Dig if tha' will, as the pigs do swill,
>   If that be thy desire.
> Or if thou'lt not, then let thy lot

>   Be famine, sword, and fire.
> Nay, man come! Breach cask and drum!
>   Share our bed and board!
> Or dost thou think this precious drink
>   Is more than thou canst afford?"

She came on with her cup again and he trembled with longing for it. Screaming with fear, the captain fled from that house. He did not stop to loose the tethered horses, but leapt upon his own and departed that place as fast as he and the horse could go.

And that is why we have this tale, for if none were left alive who would there be to tell it?

Some do say they saw a strange humped figure, bearing a sack and followed by a single file of long-handled tools, headed north, into the woods. Sure it is that nothing of value nor use was found at Dondimagia by the armies who came after. Some horses were gone, most were dead.

The beautiful crockery was smashed, the fine weavings were rotted with horribly smelling mold. Neither silver nor rubies nor any implement of iron, be it spade or scythe or pruning hook, did anyone find. All that was of bronze or brass, tin or any other metal corroded away to dust at a touch, leaving a greenish-grey powder on the profaning finger that ate away flesh to the bone and occasioned several thousands of amputations to men's sword-hands.

In the end, having nothing to dig with, except their fallen fellows' swords or their own nine fingernails, they heaped the bodies in the vast and lovely old house and set fire to it.

That fall, the vineyards grew with terrifying speed, swiftly covering the ruins, so that it was concealed from all men's sight. Grapes grow there still, but none make wine from them!

Kedorra's Kin people call the fruits of those vines, and only the birds have any joy of them.

As for Kedorra, whether or whither she went thereafter is not known to the teller of this tale, nor is it written in that Book unless some other Reader hath seen and can tell of it.

Santiago De Choch

The Goddess of Immokalee

Any sufficiently advanced technology is indistinguishable from magic.
—Arthur C. Clarke

I

I'LL NEVER GO BACK to Florida: I'll die here, in Patagonia.

I was born in Florida. Grew up in the family farm. Joined the insurgency along with my family during the war to secede. Was there, victorious, on Republic Day, Gainesville, 2036. Then met and lost the great and only love of my life before leaving the Republic of Florida as it disappeared and rejoined the other twenty-seven states in the U.S., defeated, disappointed and heartbroken. Me and Florida, both.

I grew up mostly in Spanish, with English almost entirely absent during the first four or six years of my life. German takes a third place in fluency. This story is better told in English.

I have things to teach, may teach them to a son yet, but he won't be the son I wanted, the son of Skylar Page.

My name is Rodrigo Bohn Olivares and I was born in Naples in 2020. Naples was an enclave of the very rich. I suppose it still is. My family, the Bohns, were not from there, but from Immokalee, a nearby farming town carved out of the Everglades. It supplied the Eastern U.S. with fresh produce during Northern Hemisphere winters, prime growing season for South Florida. Cattle, honey production, poultry, tropical fruit all existed, but seasonal produce was always the main business. My mother had complications leading up to my birth, and my father Carlos Bohn didn't want to risk the primitive Immokalee clinic and took her to a top Naples hospital.

In a way, my family was rich, and I was born rich. We were rich in land, tools and structures, expertise. We'd have tons of cash during good harvests, but after covering payroll for hundreds and supplies and materials to take us to the next harvest, not much remained. That's the life of the farmer. Although of course I exaggerate some. I come from old German farming stock: almost genetically disposed to saving for the future. Like the hardworking ant, a good farmer always puts something away for the harsh season, while the grasshoppers fiddle in the sun. We were never cash-rich like the Naples plutocracy, but could get the best and pay large amounts with a steady pulse when needed. The best, unfortunately, wasn't enough to save my poor mother, Antonia Olivares. She died in childbirth, so I started my life with a heavy burden. She died that I may live.

Come think of it, Skylar Page also died that I may live. Two women sacrificed themselves for me.

Although could I really call Skylar "a woman"? And was it for me only she sacrificed?

Her body was that of a woman. I found her extremely beautiful and attractive, though not perfect. Her face had something of the deer and the owl in it, something that made you look twice when you first met her, to decide if she was beautiful or just strange. Her yellow eyes could be intimidating or lovely, depending on her mood. Hair fiery red, lots of freckles, a bit too tall for a woman but not taller than me, a pleasant and well proportioned body.

However, to call her a woman would perhaps not be accurate. Men and women are born from the mix of a father and a mother's heritage; Skylar only had one parent, her father, Raymond Page. What I mean is that she was created from Mr. Page's, and only Mr. Page's, genetic stock. Her DNA was all his. Whatever combination of human traits had resulted, over millenia, in Raymond Page's stock, had become in Skylar's generation a relic, an artifact of the past, a dead language that would never again evolve or change, the language of the double helix frozen in time, endlessly replicating itself without the input of a partner. A clone.

Skylar was to be the first of a long line. A line rendered barren by design, able only to carry her father's unique human signature into the future, not just the genetic key, but his personality, memories and accumulated knowledge and malice into the future.

How could malice, or goodness for that matter, be carried into the future? How could memory, Raymond Page's feelings and recollections, be implanted in a genetic carbon copy after he had died? How could a personality survive the death of the bearer?

With Enhanced Technology, which was in its infancy then, and we fought. But it has prevailed, or at least hasn't been defeated, and we'll see what results of it. Nothing good, is my prediction. In any case, she may have been the first, but her demise didn't mean the end of occult-aided technology, not just in genetics and reproduction, but in every field you may consider: devices and networking, AI and processing power, warfare, finance, surveillance, politics. The Technology Party has triumphed not just in Florida, but in the USA and most of the world. Even this backwater, Argentina, has a *Partido Justicialista Tecnológico* government; good thing Patagonia is a backwater within a backwater, and that in this part of the world, any law, edict or mandate will be ignored if you grease the right palms or have the right contacts.

That's why I moved here when the Republic of Florida collapsed, that and the fact that a branch of the family, long lost but not quite, had settled in South Argentina when our ancestors left war-ravaged Germany after World War II, led by my great-great-grandfather, Karl Bohn, who was born in Bavaria in 1920 and arrived in Buenos Aires in 1946. His younger son, Alfonso, born Argentinian, had been restless and moved to Florida in the late 1960's to start his own farm. He was ambitious and wanted his *Lebensraum*, not crowded by older brothers who took control over most Bohn Argentinian farms after Karl died. My grandfather Peter, his sons, Lukas, Lorenzo and my father Carlos, had all been born in Immokalee. I am a third-generation Floridian, but it is my family's fate, or has been for the last hundred years, that despite our deep connection to the soil, we have had to move to different lands, and start farming anew.

My distant cousins received me with open arms when I arrived here, as defeated and destitute as my ancestor Karl Bohn had been almost a century before. But I didn't have to start from scratch. I just went from growing okra to growing apples, in a way. I had to relearn the seasons, the soils, the ways of a different farm, but I've always been a good farmer, and was still young when I arrived. I miss the mangoes and lychees, the smoked mullet, the clams, all the flavors of my Florida youth, but have come to appreciate the abundant golden wheat, the wine, and of course, the Argentinian steak grilled over coals. I've been lucky. I should have died in Florida, but I'm still alive, 30 years later. I'm grateful for that.

2

I met Skylar Page in the spring of 2039: the third growing season after Republic Day, a very busy time at the farm. Winter is the main season for most vegetables in South Florida , and we were cranking that April, at the tail end of it. Workers were in the fields before dawn, harvesting. The warehouses were packing, drying, canning and pickling twenty-four hours a day; older hens and ducks were being butchered, new flocks started, hogs and rabbits smoked and made into jerky; eggplant and jalapeño seedlings were already growing by the thousands in shadehouses in preparation for summer planting; beekeepers were harvesting the honey winter crop, and late citrus such as tangelo and grapefruit were also ripe in our grove.

Our family had always believed in putting our eggs in as many baskets as possible. That's how we survived the Old Country first, our uprootings and tribulations later. My elders had agreed we wouldn't make the mistakes that had destroyed so many other farms: switching from food crops to ornamentals for the golf courses, investing all in strawberries or sweet peppers when prices looked promising, causing market gluts and sudden catastrophic plunges, and above all, selling the land to developers. Giving in to developers and speculators had been the main mistake of many, selling not just the land but their offspring's future.

We, the Bohns, had kept our ways. Unlike so many others, we hadn't forgotten, we were now here, in a land our ancestors could never have imagined, and our farm's logo was on every cardboard box we shipped out: a smiling green bean under the Florida sun, and

Bohn Organic Farms
Immokalee, FL

in Gothic lettering under it.

I was sitting in my truck, an antique Ford Ranger, parked outside the main building of the Ponce de León University in Golden Gate, where I was an Agricultural Sciences student, going over my biology notes for an exam. I remember the sunny day and how happy I was that I could drive my truck again—we had received AGPASS/FUELCAT2 stickers, and I had placed mine covering the almost useless old yellow EDUPASS/FUELCAT6. I felt good that day, strong, confident in my lucky stars. So I had chosen music bright and dashing to go with the day: Mendelssohn's "Italian" symphony. I had prepared for the test thouroughly and wasn't worried about it. I wasn't worried about playing the symphony a bit too loudly either, windows open. Maybe the music was still illegal, I didn't know if the young Republic of Florida had gotten around to abolishing all the silly laws of the last years of State, but security surely wouldn't give me trouble about Mendelssohn.

Things were looking up for us, after years of sufferance. Farmers were important now, like never before. We had priority access to fuel and electricity. Even the president of the Republic was a farmer and a personal friend of our family, Jason Donnelly. Farmers were in charge, or we thought we were.

I saw her walking across the parking lot when I lifted my eyes from the biology notes. I'm quite sure I had not seen her before; I'd have remembered her. There was something special about her. The words "regal" and "aloof" come to mind, but that wasn't all. She seemed miles above her surroundings, lost in her own thoughts. As she walked past a group of freshman students on the lot, one of them said something and made a move towards her. She froze him in his tracks with one cold glance and kept walking.

She was headed towards her own vehicle, a much newer electric model parked at the far end of the lot despite plenty of spots available closer to the building. I realized she'd walk right past me: I should stop staring and focus on my notes. I let some time pass, then raised my eyes again looking towards her car and expecting to see her in it. She wasn't, so I looked again in the direction she had come from, and my heart skipped a beat when I saw her close and observing me with much interest and a faint, barely noticeable smile on her lips, standing a couple of feet from my side of the Ranger. I tried to do several things at once: put away the notes, which got unclipped and spilled all over my lap and onto the truck floor; turn off the music, hitting the wrong button and getting some loud Mexican music on the radio which took me several tries to kill; and saying "hello" in what I hoped would be a strong, manly voice that, to my shame, came out thin and hesitant, luckily drowned in the *corrido*. When I managed to silence the damn radio, I said "hello" again.

"Hello," she said, and I noticed her yellow eyes for the first time. "Sorry to startle you."

"Not at all, not at all."

"The music you were listening to just now, I noticed it."

I was at a loss for a moment. My grandfather had been a great influence in my life, and among other things, he had fostered a love of classical music in me. The problem was that until recently, you could have gotten in a whole lot of trouble for listening to it in public, because it was banned under the White Privilege Act, along with a lot of other things, books and such. Boy, did they give us trouble at the farm. All it took was a call to the Social Justice Police from some busybody or blackmailer. So even though times had changed, I automatically blurted out "Yes, I'm Hispanic. Do you like it, too?" Another behavior from the old times: always deny being white, and call attention upon the "Hispanic" part instead—never mind that one is always more than one thing. The world had been angry at some categories, so it was wise to claim at least two.

"No, my favorite Latin music is tango, but *corridos* is not what you were listening to. You were listening to Mendelssohn, and my question is, was it the Scottish or the Italian? It bothers me I can't place it."

I'm sure my jaw dropped for a few seconds. Outside of my immediate family, classical music had been an almost extinct art form even before the ban, as far as I knew. I managed to mumble,

"Uh, the Fourth, the Italian."

"Von Karajan?"

"I believe so, let me see," I said, found the CD case, and added, "Yes, Von Karajan with the Berlin Philharmonic."

Now she was openly smiling and giving me a strange look. Her teeth were small and looked sharp as a predator's.

"A CD, how quaint. That thing must be fifty years old, at least. The recording, much older. I have the same version in my mobile. Have you heard of them? You use them for many things like calling, texting, and oh, they hold music, too. My name is Skylar Page. What's yours?"

That was my first taste of her: ironic and straightforward, almost blunt.

"Rodrigo. Rodrigo Bohn Olivares. Nice to meet you."

"Nice meeting you too, RRRodrigo," she said, comically stretching the Spanish hard R in my name. I tried to keep her around a few more seconds:

"You're a student here, right? I don't think I've seen you before. What's your major?"

"Oh, this and that. Nothing definite. Genetics, mostly, Dr. Wu's class. You're in Ag Science, right?"

"Yes. How did you ...?"

"The truck. The stickers on the truck. Your hands. It's obvious."

I had to smile. Man, she was sharp. Beautiful, and sharp.

"I'd like to ... hm, could we maybe meet some other time? We can talk about music. Maybe we could ..."

"Yes, maybe we could, RRRodrigo," she said, "I'm sure I'll see you around. Do you help at Ms. Gonzalez' garden?"

"Yes!"

"I've been meaning to check it out. I'll see you there sometime. *Me voy. Hasta luego.*"

"Do you speak Spanish?"

"*Muy mal. Nos vemos.*"

She walked away and I stared as she started her car and silently glided by, waving a hand as she did. The stickers on it were white, and the black lettering read ETCORPPASS/FUELCAT1+. Trumped mine. She could get recharged anywhere, anytime, and breeze past most SEC roadblocks. A few seconds later, another late model vehicle followed, two burly men in it. One of them gave me the briefest nod as they drove by, then typed something in the screenpad he was holding. As they drove away, I saw the SECPASS black stickers, and, much smaller, the Screaming Eagle emblem. These guys were no Ponce de León campus sec dummies. They were 101st Airborne, one of the toughest — and most expensive — security franchises. Then I realized I'd be late for the test, rushed into my classroom — stopping for just a second at the door for the facial recog system to register me and the green light to flash — sat down, and took it. I got a C.

3

My father had insisted I attend Ag Science classes at the nearby, nonprofit Ponce de León University, in many ways more of a trade school than a college. At the demo farm, frankly, I taught more than learned, due to my lifelong farming background. Ms. Gonzalez, a stout, strong older Guatemalan, ran the two-acre demo farm competently, despite not having any education at all. She was illiterate, which is by no means the same as ignorant. I was happy to be useful and help her train a new generation of growers. The Republic needed them desperately. As a child, she had started helping her dirt-poor family tend to the traditional *milpa* of corn, beans and squash ("the three sisters" of the original cultures throughout the Americas), and had come into the U.S. as a teenager, paying a coyote to guide her and her twin sister with her family's accumulated savings, and the promise of more as soon as she was in *El Norte*.

She had survived the passage, her sister hadn't. She then worked like a mule for decades in the fields of Immokalee, saving every penny to send back home after the smuggler was paid off. I knew this because she had been a worker at our farm in her later years, before we insisted she should now quit the fields. She couldn't be idle, though, and my father had come up with the inspired idea of insinuating her to the dean of Ponce de León, who set up the demo garden for her as part of the curriculum. Our family was a major donor to the university, which accounts for "suggestions" from the Bohn clan enacted quickly. This one had been particularly good. She was in her element.

I can clearly remember Skylar Page as she walked past the gate that first time at Ms. Gonzalez's garden: wearing faded work clothes, baggy jeans and a long-sleeved shirt, all in clear colors, and a big hat, which is exactly what you wear when you work outside in Florida, with its murderous sun and myriads of no-see-ums, mosquitoes and fire ants ready to chew you up. Ms. Gonzalez made a beeline towards her, walking as fast as her advanced age would allow, and let loose a stream of angry Spanish. I was working the worm bins with a few others some distance away from the gate, and could only catch a word here and there, "late," "didn't sign up."

Skylar let the old gardener rant awhile, then soothingly spoke to her in hushed, respectful tones. Finally she pointed to rows of chard and collards that needed weeding, and moved to the side to let Skylar walk there. As she passed my group, she shot me an amused glance, but didn't stop or talk to me.

I was pleased to see her weeding like a pro, at a steady pace, pulling up the weeds with roots and all. I could see she was making a good impression on Ms. Gonzalez, who was famously cranky: she'd look in her direction now and then, and then go back to harvesting clusters of Everglades tomatoes, a satisfied expression on her wrinkled dark face under the battered sombrero she always wore.

The brief coolness of winter had already faded away: the heat seemed to start earlier and earlier every year. Soon, Skylar was covered in sweat like the rest of us, but she never stopped her work or asked for water. It was Ms. Gonzalez herself who brought her a glass from the cool water jug after an hour, and that told me she had accepted the newcomer. She liked to see what kind of worker one was before offering water, so she could dismiss the useless ones when they asked: "*Sí*, go drink *agua*, and don't come back, *pendejo*."

Hours passed; everybody finished one chore and moved to the next under Ms. Gonzalez's stern direction. At long last, she stopped working, took a long drink of water, straightened her back, and looked in the direction of the sun, now sinking in the west, towards the Gulf of Mexico. She clapped her hands a few times, which was the signal for us to go put our tools back in the shed and leave.

As the shadows darkened, some went to the hand-cranked water pump to splash their arms and faces, and Ms. Gonzalez disappeared inside her cabin: she lived on the garden grounds, in a small cabin beside the shed. Soon, light appeared on the single window, and I could hear the rattling of dishes as she started preparing her dinner. I stood next to Skylar as she finished refreshing herself at the water pump, my desire for her strong.

Then she somehow ditched her bodyguards and came to spend the night with me.

We entered my land through one of the south gates, as I always did. Dogs started barking some distance away, and soon a pack of them approached the truck at speed. I slowed down and put my arm out of the window so they could smell it. Trotting behind them, two farm workers on night watch duty waved at me as I came to a stop.

"*Buenas noches, don Rodrigo,*" the oldest one said, and took his straw hat off.

"*Buenas noches, Camilo. Todo bien?*"

"*Sí, señor.*"

I told them that I had my corner of the land covered and they could go guard the other end of that fence, miles away. They had dogs, machetes, and an old shotgun. Their job was less to deter well armed intruders than to alert the farm of any breaching of the fence, and deal with poachers.

I drove the rough path edged by palmetto and pine before turning into neat rows of mango trees and then field after field, some still bearing winter produce, others newly planted or tilled, and some in fallow, planted with green manures: cowpeas, buckwheat.

Gradually my cabin, where I had lived alone since age fourteen, became visible, and we heard the barking of my dog, Beckenbauer, a big German shepherd jumping at the fence, happy to see me. *"Ruhig sein, Beckenbauer! Stille machen! Legen, Beck!"* Beck was a guard dog and looked it. He had scars from old fights with coons and hogs, and from a time when he had held a madman with a machete in place for several minutes until help could arrive. As I was unlatching my gate, I heard Skylar get out of the truck, and Beck shot straight to her, bypassing me. He sniffed her extended hand for a moment, then licked it, and she smiled.

"You're not afraid of him. Most people are."

"Such a good dog. Why Beckenbauer?"

"Best defender ever. Bayern Munich and the fearsome *Mannschaft*. Before my time, but I have the videos."

"Only speaks German?"

"Spanish and English, too," I said, smiling.

I turned the lights of my small cabin on, then we walked through the old citrus grove outside, to the outdoor kitchen and shed.

"It's pretty. What's that?" she asked, pointing to another structure some distance away, surrounded by thick cocoplums.

"Outhouse and shower. There's a sink and a mirror in there, if you need to use it."

"I'd love a shower, RRRodrigo. Ms. Gonzalez made me sweat today."

"No hot water, I'm out of propane."

"I never use hot water."

"Ah, okay, let me, um, turn the light on and check for spiders."

"Never mind that. I'm not afraid. Haven't you noticed? Of anything. It's a curse I have."

"Why is that a curse?"

"It's gotten me into a lot of trouble. Do you have fresh towels in there?"

"No, they're inside. Let me go get some."

I came back, saw the light of the shower room was still off. I knocked. "I have some towels here. Let me get the light for you. It's hard to find."

"Come in," she said. I stepped in. There was enough moonlight to see her, standing naked, looking at me without a word. Her skin was very white, with lots of freckles in some places. She raised an arm, beckoning me to join her. I dropped the towels and embraced her, finding her mouth ready for my kiss. Soon, we were madly aroused. "Protection," I whispered; "No need," she answered. I pushed her against the wall and went into her. She made some strange noises as she climaxed, like birds cooing or owls calling. An owl actually answered the call from somewhere in the trees, outside.

4

After that night, we started seeing each other every time we could, spending nights at my cabin after demo farm days. Spring turned into summer, and with it, a great heaviness set on the land. The rhythms and routines of the farm changed with the season. There are different things to grow all year round in Florida. Days had to start earlier, to take advantage of the cooler hours. By noon, bells and loudspeakers told the workers in the fields to seek shelter, and they slowly walked to their dwellings, to hammocks in deep shade, under the gaze of the sun, blank and pitiless, as Skylar often observed. Towards late afternoon, peasants would return to work. The sun was less cruel by then, but other tortures awaited: swarms of biting insects, and an oppressive humidity that would often break into violent storms. We lost four workers to lighting bolts. That summer of 2039 would also witness an explosion of dangerous creatures that seemed to lurk under every rotten log and dark corner: water moccasins and coral snakes, widow and recluse spiders claimed the lives of more Immokalee residents, and especially of their young children, than in any other summer in memory.

To add to our woes, and despite our own best efforts and those of local authorities and churches, famine had set on the land. Immokalee and Homestead, the main farming hubs for southwest and southeast Florida respectively, both had to mobilize their militias to keep the desperate out. There simply wasn't enough food and shelter for everyone. Gainesville, the new capital, sent aid caravans, big, slow trucks, loaded with peanuts and potatoes and guarded by few, second-rate troops, as many as could be spared as the northern border had to be secured against raids from Washington. But they seldom made it south of Orlando: wild-eyed, skeletal mobs ambushed them. The walled enclaves of the wealthy in Naples and West Palm were well provisioned, and elite troops guarding them didn't hesitate to open fire on the hungry crowds when they tried to push in. Giant Chinook cargo helicopters from those places landed at the farm weekly, and loaded bushels of summer crops, sweet potatoes, eggplants, and okra, along with crates of live chickens and rabbits. Machine-gunners sometimes opened fire on the crowds begging at our gates while flying out, just for sport. We hated them. Their firepower was far superior, and we couldn't risk a confrontation, so we supplied them, made sure our population and workers were fed, and gave what little remained to churches to distribute to the hungry. My father had decided that was the only possible course of action. This decision weighed heavily on him.

The road from Naples to Ponce de León was kept clear by seasoned mercenaries with armored vehicles, and patrolled by killer drones. Most of the companies guarding the Naples road were franchises owned by Raymond Page's FloTech: NYPD, Marines, Rangers. Her bodyguards were elite 101st Airborne

Iran vets. On the Immokalee side, the Madariagas, a clan involved in many activities legal and not, guaranteed security. I had talked to Frankie, the head of the clan and a family friend, about Skylar, so she could come and go as she pleased.

My father and uncles didn't like all this, but let us be. I was on the cusp of becoming like them, an equal, a full grown man and leader. My decisions were to be respected, if not liked. That much had become clear in June, as the full council of family, farm foremen, regional allies, and militia captains convened.

Perhaps because of our youth, Skylar and I found it possible to forget the terrible scenes happening all around us when we were together. My cabin and grove were an oasis where, week after week, we got to know each other more intimately. We'd make love, take cold showers, turn on the small AC unit in the cabin as a special luxury. We'd smoke hand-rolled cigars from the farm, or the better, Cuban ones smuggled in by the Madariagas, swinging in hammocks under the shade of trees, pick mangoes and get sticky eating them. Best days of my life.

We would lie in bed exhausted after lovemaking, and sometimes, especially at first, she would talk of the simplest things, of her love for all animals or her favorite recipes. She'd recite long paragraphs of poetry and drama from memory: Blake, Shakespeare, Yeats were her favorites.

But as time passed, and our intimacy progressed, she would absentmindedly mention earth-shattering things. Things that fell outrageously outside my field of experience, things I couldn't imagine. Hard-to-understand things, explained by her as she lay in the hammock if the no-see-ums were not too bad, cigar in hand. "There's a new science now, a hyper-science, preparing to become the religion it has always wanted to be," she'd start. The corporations in control of it had come to a commercially-friendly tag, "ET," for its vague name of "enhanced technology," and it was now represented by a powerful political party too, the TP, Technology Party. "Gatekeeper scientist *brujos* are making deals with what's beyond the gates, sponsored by tycoons like my father."

Over the course of many nights that summer, it became clear to me that Skylar hated the abuse and murder of human beings inherent to the art of magi since remote times. A fair number of humans had been murdered to create her. Deities had been propitiated, energies released. Deals made, Faustian deals.

I write from a backwater, and the waves of change spread slowly and may not fully reach us here for decades to come, hopefully. I don't know if a hypothetical future reader will be aware of some of the things I'm talking about here, so let me be clear: I don't mean voluntary or involuntary tissue and organ donors. Or the many abused and murdered during the extended research that led to a first Vessel, Skylar Page. There was a fair number of both, but those were deaths in the name of science. Deaths manageable in public discourse, if more or less disapprovingly. What I'm saying is that enhanced technology requires human sacrifice, as well as other offerings such as animal and self-sacrifice. So there's a category of people who died so that Skylar would be, who died not for science, but for a whole field of knowledge not only separate, but denied, unfathomable by science. Until recently, say until around the time I was born, and Skylar was "born," in 2020.

Despite my youth back when this story happens, I already was responsible for hundreds of lives, for tasks of enormous significance like achieving a good crop or protecting it from raiders. I was no stranger to life-and-death decisions. I had been in the Florida War, president Jason Donnelly was a personal friend of my family, and we had all been at his inaguration after fighting on his side. In a word: except for the natural awkwardness and stupidity of youth, I was no simpleton. The Bohns were not billionaires like the Naples and Miami cartels, but we fed a lot of people in times when food was scarce, we held territorial power and a degree of military capabilities in the form of our Farm & County Militia, and we were in politics too, in the Farmers Party that ultimately lost the battle for Florida. Despite all this, I had a hard time understanding her. My horror was met with her matter-of-factness, a cold delivery of facts too awful to contemplate.

I think now that she had a premonition. She knew she didn't have long to live. Didn't want to live long. That's why she opened up to me so fast and so thoroughly. Above all, she didn't want to be her father's Vessel. The many rich and powerful striving to create their own Vessels to migrate into before death, adding a lifetime, potentially many lifetimes, to the one that was theirs to spend, should take heed of the fact that the first unfortunate born into that situation rejected it with heart and soul. "Glitches," the technicians will say, "that have been fixed in the new releases," but I don't doubt that at least some of the new race are conspiring as I write this, irate and Luciferian in their hatred of the soulless men and bloodthirsty energies bringing them to life, possibly bent not just on taking their revenge on the "mothers" and "fathers" conjuring them into existence, but on the whole lot of us, guilty and innocent alike. And who could blame them?

5

As I had promised my elders, I didn't let this love affair, my first, interfere with my responsibilities. I'd be up hours before dawn and head off to work after a cup of black, scalding coffee, leaving her sleeping in my bed. When I could, I'd be back for a few hours in the middle of the day, then go out again. Coming back in the dark, I'd stop to deliver dinner from the main farmhouse kitchen to the men guarding my road and gate, then drive on and see the lights of the outdoor kitchen lit, Skylar putting the finishing touches on our dinner, with Beckenbauer laying under the ceiling fan, lovingly watching her. When this happened, the times that she came to stay with me, I felt a warmth inside, a feeling of happiness, of the possibility of a life together, a family.

"What are you cooking?" I'd say, pouring us some farm mead or starfruit wine.

"Poor man's caviar. It's a recipe I brought from my student days in Europe. It's ready. Here, try it," she said, dipped a piece of our coarse bread in it, and put it in my mouth.

"It's good! Is this the eggplants I brought earlier?"

"Yes! You bake them whole, until soft, along with sweet peppers. Then put all that to sweat in a covered dish until it cools. That makes the skins easy to remove. Chop everything real fine with a knife, and add some lemon juice, raw garlic, salt, a pinch of sugar, and plenty of olive oil and red vinegar. *Voilà!*"

Her green-yellow eyes were full of joy as she explained all this, and the joy was contagious. She looked beautiful, with her red hair tied in a ponytail, and the eggplant dip tasted like home. I had never tried it before, but it tasted like home. I include the recipe here because she always said it's what she wanted to be remembered for.

6

Another time during summer rainy season, we were driving the truck along cattle pastures, and she pointed at the mushrooms growing on piles of cow manure, spindly and light-colored. "What are those?" she asked.

"Psilocybes, *cucumelos*."

"That's what I thought! Stop the truck, let's pick some!"

"Are you sure? I haven't had one in years, they can be powerful."

"Yes!"

We picked about a dozen of the best, and drove back. After washing them, we sliced and sprinkled them with a little salt. We ate some, washing them down with big gulps of water. Their powerful effect soon became apparent. As the sunlight faded, we took a walk in the grove surrounding my cabin. We giggled and were silly for a while, but the next stage of the high took over soon, and we became more pensive, observing the world around us. We talked about what we were seeing in our altered state of mind, but words were not enough to describe the luminous sap flowing from the roots, through the trunk and branches of every tree, until reaching the tiniest capillary in the foliage. We tried to talk about the bright tendrils of energy emanating from every plant and creating an amazing network that breathed and pulsated. We tried to describe the entities we perceived all around us, some tiny, some massive, tried to describe our feeling of being observed by them, of now being in their plane of existence, intruders in their world. We didn't feel threatened by them, but knew we were being watched as we left the grove and walked towards the wild scrub of pine and palmetto in complete darkness, not tripping or stumbling once, our bodies somehow navigating the starlit night without problem. "Yes," she said, "this is another way for the third eye to open," and then we both fell silent. Speaking had become difficult, our mouths felt swollen and dry, so we started conversing telepathically without realizing it. The thought of a snake or any other danger didn't cross our minds once, and so those dangers never appeared.

For once in the rainy season, it was a clear night, and the east sky started palpitating with a glow, growing lighter until it birthed a bright, rising moon. The world became brighter, and I looked at Skylar's face: it was white and translucent, tiny veins visible under the skin, carrying minute amounts of blood that moved in unison with her heartbeat. Her mouth was crimson, her eyes completely yellow now and very bright. Moths were circling her head like satellites, but as I focused my attention on them, I realized they were not moths but fairies, tiny winged humanlike figures having an animated conversation with her as they flew around her head, which was becoming brighter every minute.

I felt something tug at my legs and looked down, and there was a very short, dark-skinned, naked, old man with a white beard, not taller than my knees' height, looking up at me and smiling. He made a fist, waved it and, without opening his mouth, still smiling, said to me, "Be strong! ¡Sé fuerte! Sei stark!" in my three languages simultaneously. I smiled back at him. The moon was high when I looked at Skylar again, and the moths, or fairies, were gone. She was looking at me, and her jewel-like eyes said, "I want to show you a vision." An image appeared inside my skull, grew larger, and soon occupied my whole field of vision: at first I thought I was seeing a multitude of ants moving around an anthill, but then I realized I was flying above charred terrain. Fires were burning, and columns of smoke rose up all around me as I flew. The moving figures were not ants but thousands of people. They were taking other people towards a pyramid, and dragging them to the top. I flew closer and saw the scene at the summit, which was flat. Naked and covered in blood, wearing masks, men were busy sacrificing prisoners as they reached the platform. Four masked figures held the captives' limbs and spread them on stone altars, as a fifth one ripped open their chests and elevated the beating hearts towards the sky for a moment, before tossing them onto smoking braziers.

I realized I had been hearing powerful drums only when they fell silent. I looked everywhere to discover the cause of the sudden silence, and saw all faces were raised towards me. I would be discovered! I sensed a massive presence behind me, and turning around, my blood froze when I saw a giant emerging from a hole in the charred ground, cloaked in smoke. Its monstrous head was covered in scales and oozed blood, its eyes were dead and dark, and even though I was flying high, it was already almost level with me as I recoiled in horror. The mouth slowly opened, and as flocks of black birds flew all around it, crowing and cackling, a long tongue unfurled, almost reaching the creature's chest. Inside the mouth, I could see human skulls by the hundreds, many with rotten flesh and eyeballs still attached to them. A piercing, loud wail filled the air, and a deadly stench, and as the giant started raising an arm towards me, fear filled my heart, and I started falling in a downward corkscrew motion, my flying powers gone. I screamed in terror, and the scene disappeared: I was lying on the ground, my head on Skylar's lap. The world was dark again, the moon had set. Her face was sweet and her eyes bright as she caressed me like a mother rescuing her child from a nightmare. "You have to help me. I can't do it alone. I need you to help me stop this," she said, and I lost consciousness.

7

Raymond Page intended to occupy his Vessel on her nineteenth birthday, October 31st.

"Don't ask the questions if you're afraid of the answers," she said, but that statement was itself a question: "Are you afraid to know?" And of course I was. The revelations about who she was and what was going on in the Naples labs were horrifying. The reality of the new Republic in the summer of 2039 was discouraging too, but I didn't have the luxury to be paralyzed by fear. I had to hold, or the center wouldn't. Our lives would be blown away by the hurricanes, metaphorical and real, that kept coming at us, howling. But the terrors of my world were squared, cubed, in hers. Her lovely body, the soft skin that I adored, contained a maelstrom of horrors compared to which the brutality of South Florida was commonplace and not that scary, really.

Yes, shortly after that visionary night, the hurricanes had started coming at us, one after another, like never before. Category 4 or above, every single one, and unnaturally numerous. Making a dire situation much, much worse with wanton death and destruction, lost crops, flattened structures, drowned animals, dead people. "Don't ask the questions if you're afraid of the answers." We were sheltering that night in my childhood room in the enormous farmhouse, the sturdiest structure for miles around. My brother and uncles, and their families, as well as many workers and foremen, as many as could be taken in, were there too, the rest of them sheltering in basements and warehouses around the land.

My father, grim, brow deeply furrowed, sat in the cavernous dining room, every window covered and reinforced with plywood and sheet metal, listening to the emergency radio. Every so often, he would crank the handle to recharge it, then pour himself a drink and walk to the main door, open it a crack, peer outside, and come back. My grandmother and aunts supervised the kitchen staff, and a meal was served as the fiercest bands of the storm started hitting us. Despite the thick brick walls, we could hear the raging, murderous winds outside. A flying object hit the house every few minutes, heavier and heavier objects, uprooted trees, farm equipment, dead animals. Water trickled under every door and from the ceilings as the hurricane brought torrential rains. My father had lost contact with other points at the farm, and only occasionally would pick up the government frequency from Gainesville, amid bursts of static: "... life-threatening conditions ... storm surge expected to flood coastal areas ... all interests north of Chokoloskee and south of Punta Gorda should now shelter in place ..."

The meal was served, more candles were lit, and dozens of us bowed our heads as my father said grace. "You send us many trials, Lord. One after another they come, yet we don't lose faith. We're hit, and hit again and again, but we stay strong. We don't give in to despair but stand and fight. Many depend on us, in this house, this farm, this town, and this Republic. We don't pray to be spared. We pray for strength. Amen," he said, "Amen," everybody answered. I admired him that night, the way he said his simple prayer, holding his head high, his full beard jutting ahead as if in defiance of the neverending wave of misfortune and trouble.

Nobody said much during dinner, and when it was over, the family, along with some guests who had taken refuge with us, retired to the music room, where tea and liquors were served. Skylar, who had not said much until then, raised her *kirsch schnapps* and said, "To a great family and a grand tradition, to the noblest of all calls: making things grow and feeding us all. Thank you for your hospitality tonight. *Prost! ¡Salud!*" Then she approached my father and asked him something quietly. He looked at her for an instant, surprised, and then nodded. She sat at the old piano that had been in the family since Germany, and played music for us. Chopin mostly, Grieg, and Beethoven, as the hurricane raged outside.

Later, in my childhood room, I woke up feeling observed. Her eyes were fixed on me with intensity. She seemed to be waiting for me to say something, waiting in deep silence, not willing to push me but expecting, hoping I'd say the right thing. The storm was finally subsiding outside. I mustered the courage to talk to her.

"Skylar, the other night, with the mushrooms ... the scene you showed me. What was it? How did you do that."

"Don't ask the questions if you're afraid of the answers."

"I'm not. Tell me."

8

Humans had forever interacted with chthonic entities. Some families had historically been mediums and sorcerers, passing their knowledge of magic and the ritual abuse it sometimes demanded down to their younger generations, for centuries and, in a few cases, millennia. Dark knowledge was hard to obtain, but the results were real. The bloodline known as Page in its current iteration was one of the savviest and most ruthless. Their initial payment of knowledge had been from the force known as Moloch, in return for tributes of children's suffering at its temples on the Mediterranean coast, three thousand years ago. Then the bloodline had increased it over many generations, in Egypt, Asia Minor, and Rome, slowly migrating to Celtic Europe, becoming Chiefs and Druids, going underground when the Cross prevailed, and embarking for America with the first waves of settlers. They had been in their element as soon as they arrived, because, as Burroughs famously said and Skylar quoted, "America is not a young land: it is old, and dirty, and evil. Before the settlers, before the Indians, the evil was there ... waiting."

Power demands more power. And the gods can give some in exchange for life forces spent to feed them, but are reluctant to give so much that their worshippers will become their equals, and start gobbling up their due. When fiefdoms and empires built around gods collapse, and the stream of sacrifices and adoration dwindles, so dwindle the gods. They slowly shrink back to their original shape and true importance as sovereigns of a particular spring, grove, or mountain. They only rule over a few snakes or jaguars, and are reduced to surviving on the mice they hunt. After ruling over populous cities and vast territories with their far more richly tithing human populations, this is a painful withdrawal for them. Legacy streams of life force still flowing to them through myths, dreams, and the residual terror and awe of a disappearing culture also fade away as the culture is forgotten, making their torture worse.

The power that comes from tribute is their drug and fuel, and they will go to great extremes to stay connected to the feeding tube, increasing, Skylar's ancestors noticed, their knowledge allowances to whoever will guarantee a steady supply of power and tribute.

Raymond Page's namesake grandfather was the one who had made the breakthrough: "The gods are junkies. If we play our cards right, and get them truly addicted, they'll make concessions. They'll give us more and more of what makes them gods every time we shut the spigot. They'll suffer in agony and grant us what we want. And what we want is to become them, to replace them, but we need to hide that purpose until we are strong and can defeat them."

So for three generations now, the Pages had been providing the gods with richer nourishment. They had worked tirelessly to develop new vehicles of delivery for the gods' high. Torture and ritual sacrifice had increased, both in quantity and quality, but other streams had been created: software inserted in popular apps from almost the beginning of the digital age magically fed them spoonfuls of the souls of millions glued to their screens. Messages and incantations in popular film, music and television likewise resulted in slow degradation of their consumers, with every ounce of life force lost migrating to the Gods' fund. Vast energies could be gathered by sowing the seeds of fear and hatred among different populations, when those populations engaged in conflict.

She explained that the bloodthirsty gods didn't give a fig about Gaia (the only goddess she accepted) except as the field to grow their human crop upon, to be kept profitable and productive as a farm, producing by intensive use of poisons, without regard for the soil's long-term health, or for the goodness of the fruits it bears. Not just that: Skylar's philosophy was in great part the study of how massive sacrifices required massive resources, and of how tired and angry Gaia was. It's not only that the millions to die for the abominations had to live, eat and shit before their sacrifice. It's that the millions needed to have screens if they were to channel their energy through them, and entertainments, and consumer goods, to keep them happy and stupefied.

Gaia, Skylar said, had told her that the only way to restore balance would be to fallow most of the Earth, especially the areas around "the biggest mouths": openings to the realms of deities especially old, huge, gluttonous, and malevolent. The Yucatán, Haiti, the deserts of Arizona, Sonora and Chihuahua, and Tenochtitlán (Mexico City) had hosted the hungriest gods for the longest time, and ET had brought them back hungrier than ever. The only way for them to be pushed back into their "mouths" again would be to starve them of tribute for centuries, to let Nature slowly take over and restore peace. Some humans could remain, as long as they accepted their limits and didn't try to build empires or reawaken the Gods, but most would have to go.

She agonized over the question of who would have to carry on Gaia's will. Humans alone couldn't. In supporting the natural human impulse to propagate and be many, cunning observers, like her father, aware of the value that a head of cattle holds for the cattleman, swam with the demographic flow, pleasing populations with the promise of a New Order without hunger or strife, if only they could be allowed to take over - if dissenting voices and those not bending to the robot and the Golem, to Moloch and Tláloc, were eliminated.

I sometimes could see a cloud darken Skylar's face even in joyous moments, and I knew she was coming to the conclusion that she would have to do her part. She was already engaged in mild efforts at depopulation. She had used her access privileges and stealthily sabotaged operations here and there. Chip brain implant facilities, device battery assembly lines, chemical factories had been attacked with arson, hacking, even magic, by her and her ecoterrorist associates. The uber-rich men of the Naples compounds checking into elite clinics to have a penis enlargement would get an unscheduled vasectomy into the bargain. Their wives going for breast augmentation surgery would receive tainted silicone, slowly releasing agents that would kill the carrier within a year. Skylar was instrumental in aiding Dr. Wu, FloTech's Chief Science Officer (and a professor of genetics as a way to scout for young bright minds), in pursuing his parallel, illicit lines of research. On the human side, at least. How Dr. Wu managed to fool the entities that had to be present when certain spells were cast in the labs as new and more potent forms of bioengineering emerged, she didn't know. "He must be a very powerful magician," she said.

It was Dr. Wu who procured the weapons and reconnoitered for these guerrilla missions, sterilizing a few, eliminating others, putting a hiccup in the machine by disabling an assembly line for some time; but he, and Skylar herself, knew that this wasn't enough by a long shot. More radical action was needed if they were to have a chance at winning. And what would winning look like? "The biggest mouths" rendered mute and unable to feed by depriving them of "the small mouths" of human populations around them.

9

As fall began, I collaborated in one of those efforts. A shipment of beans and okra had to be inoculated with a certain bacterium. The crop was destined for some lower-middle-class areas of Naples. Their inhabitants thought that they lived in a modern, well run world. They thought they had jobs, entering numbers into screens, marketing VR games, or selling alligator purses to the shoppers at gated malls surrounded by famished masses and the environmental disaster that most of South Florida was. Skylar and Dr. Wu explained the real purpose of those roughly two thousand people: they were kept alive solely as part of a pool, one of many, of sacrificial victims. Screen time was kept cheap and plentiful in those quarters, social interactions in the real world discouraged in many ways, so when a FOR SALE sign appeared in the yard—all identical in their green lawns—the neighbors were happy with FloTech's explanation: the owners had been offered job upgrades out of town, and accepted. "Of course," the neighbors, who also worked for some FloTech outfit, would say, "who wouldn't?"

This was awful, but how was it my job to do anything about it? "Don't think you are safe," Dr. Wu said, and Skylar sadly nodded from her perch behind him. "You and your family are given a pass now because you're useful. At some point, you won't be anymore. This is what will come to you, this or worse. Watch," he said as he sat by one of the computer terminals and placed his hand on the screen for access. We were at one of FloTech's many research facilities, after-hours, and everything glowed white except for the massive, black processing units lining a wall, performing billions of operations every second. He typed, and a video came up; Skylar pushed me gently from behind to make me approach Dr. Wu and watch what he was showing me. I wish I hadn't. A room very much like this one, with identical CPUs along a wall, although the equipment seemed different. I can't really describe what the purpose of that facility was, but what I did see was a group of maybe ten teenaged naked boys and girls on racks, being flayed alive by what looked like furry midgets or apes wearing headresses of antlers. "They thought they were safe, too. Nobody is. Do you know what they died for? Officially, a bus accident. In real fact, they died for the secret of a better night-vision system, a minor improvement in one of FloTech's bioluminescence-based, heat-seeking, mixed-reality-capable vision aids. Records show that eighty-five abductees from the Airport Road Villages in total were ... used in this way to achieve version 3.2 of these goggles. Understand, Mr. Bohn: these people are bred like chickens. We will be doing them a favor by ending their lives ahead of time and without torture, neh?"

I still doubted, as Dr. Wu pierced me with a somber gaze, but Skylar whispered in my ear: "Remember what the mushroom showed you; if the Beast is starved, the pyramid will crumble and fall, and the murderers on the top will fall with it."

So I agreed to become a murderer myself, arranging to have the crop left in a warehouse under my control overnight, and dusting the tubs of produce with the contents of a tube. Airport Road Villages was wiped out. FloTech and local government announced a new virus that killed people suddenly in their sleep had been discovered in the water, and gave all others in neighboring communities placebo vaccinations against it, and that was that. They knew it had been ecoterrorism, magic-terrorism. What they didn't know is that it had been hatched from the inside. Now I shared some of Skylar's burden, perhaps the best definition of love.

Famine outside the gated compounds was getting more acute every week as bird and frog populations declined, fish and most mammals having been eaten a long time ago. Bohn Farms was preparing massive plantings for the upcoming season, the biggest ever. All resources were being pushed to the limit, and I moved around my days in a daze, sending crews to till this field, plant the other. Civil war was breaking out again in Florida, and this second time, the Technology Party was aligning itself with Washington and they had the advantage. The raids on Immokalee were getting more intense every week, and we needed a good harvest in the winter.

I loved Skylar, but hated her too. I now knew so much more than I had wanted to: oppressive knowledge, the stuff of nightmares. It seemed to me now I had lived my whole life in a nightmare, but never understanding it for what it was, spared the details. The doors of perception had now been opened, and I resented this, resented it deeply. I was now a terrorist and murderer, hiding things from my family, privy to despairing knowledge. A happy future for us had seemed a possibility before; now, that prospect was dead.

The prevailing feeling was that nobody would come out alive and unhurt in Florida, us least of all. Time was running short for her. To flee was impossible. Magical forces too powerful to hide from could be summoned and would find her anywhere. The only option was to fight. But how?

At this point, in early October, I had a long meeting with my father, and opened my heart to him. Everything I'm telling here, the story of my time with Skylar and the things I had learned from her, even my shameful tainting of a crop bearing the family seal, all was revealed. I had no right to keep it to myself. This was terrible knowledge that Clan and Farm had to have. I didn't know whether Skylar would take it as a betrayal, but I had to put my own on alert. By the time I left his house with the first sun, his hair, which had been gray, was white.

10

The following night, as I was lying in bed with Skylar, I was awaken by the sound of horses approaching. I jumped and armed myself, bidding Skylar to stay in the room; she followed me, holding Beckenbauer by the collar. As we stepped outside, we saw it was no danger; my own guards and watchmen were respectfully opening the gate for my father, my brother and uncles, and their escort bearing Kalashnikovs in the saddles and knives and revolvers on their belts, a dozen men stern and gloomy. My father dismounted and walked towards us, as one of my laborers held his horse and led it to water. He looked at Skylar for a very long time, and nobody moved or said anything during that. Then he turned his eyes in my direction and spoke:

"The times are hard, son. You need to tell them what you told me last night. Or better yet, the *señorita* should."

Without looking at her, I knew Skylar had been surprised. It only took her a second to understand. She had been standing back, but approached me now, and looking at my father in the eye, said:

"*Adelante, don Carlos,*" extending an arm to invite them to the outside kitchen, which had a big wooden table that could sit us all. "*Señores, adelante, por favor. ¿Van a querer café y licores?*"

"*Café solamente, gracias,*" he answered, and sent his guards, and mine, to establish a perimeter and wait outside. Cigars were passed around, and Skylar appeared with a pot of fragrant coffee. We all sipped it. I noticed none of my kin was visibly armed, a sign of respect for my house. We all waited for my father to speak first:

"Rodrigo, señorita Skylar, forgive us for coming to you like this. The times force us to it, and the bad news. Gainesville has fallen."

"Where's Donnelly? Is he retreating with the troops?"

"He's dead, son. And most of his troops, too. Washington's dropped a tactical nuke on Gainesville."

"Some of the troops remain," explained my uncle Lukas, who looked like one of the motorcycle gangsters of yore with his long gray braided beard and leather vest. "Ocala is being mobilized, Lake O and Orlando, Tampa. Florida is not yet defeated. Your father has been designated president, Rodrigo."

"I don't know what to say ... you surely don't want congratulations."

"No, he doesn't," said Lorenzo. "He shouldn't have accepted. It's hopeless. We can't fight them. We should be able to come to terms in exchange for safe passage. The Madariagas could arrange getting us to Cuba."

"How can you speak like that?" I interrupted. "We have to fight! You have no idea of what the Technology Party really is. There's no coming to terms, uncle! It's us or them! They will show no mercy!"

"Exactly!" he yelled in a voice full of fear. He was thin, nervous and bald. "Us or them! And do you think it will be us? They just dropped an atomic bomb on us, fool!"

Slowly, my father rose: "¡Silencio! Miss Page, you understand the risk, our dilemma in sitting you at the table and making you privy to our considerations. You surely see we will have to come to an understanding, you and us, tonight. If we can't, we'll have to take you hostage."

11

"That, don Carlos, wouldn't be a bad idea," Skylar said. "I see Rodrigo has opened your eyes to parts of reality that nobody wants to visit, and I apologize for shattering a part of all of you by knowledge of the true state of affairs. It's all true. Unbelievable and true. Father knows of my love for Rodrigo," she continued. "I was careful to let him know, to feign an intent for secrecy while dropping some hints around the right ears. This may be the sole reason your farm hasn't been attacked yet. He could take it anytime he wanted it, but it will cost him troops, which are needed elsewhere as new war visits Florida."

"You're damn right it would cost him troops," uncle Lukas said darkly, stroking his beard.

"He's thinking, 'Why fight for the farm, when I can take it through marriage?' So he, my friends, is thinking of marrying Rodrigo. He intends to take what's his this Halloween. He will live in what I was, and I will be no more," she said, and hung her head. I rushed to embrace her. "Not if I can stop it!"

"War is coming to Bohn Farms, one way or another. He will either conquer it by force, or conquer it by treachery when the families are joined in marriage."

Skylar rose from her seat, eyes glowing and terrible: "So I say let's bring war to him now, when he's weak and not expecting it! Surrender is death, there's no place for the weak in the world that's coming! Raymond Page has something he very much wants, or rather, he doesn't have it if I'm your hostage. Time is ticking. Halloween's close. So we can force his hand to our advantage, if we're bold."

Slowly don Carlos rose, and looking at Lorenzo said: "I think Miss Skylar speaks wisely. I say she's one of us now. We will survive, or perish, together. Fighting. Now is the time to agree, or disagree, with my judgment, and face the consequences." He kept staring at Lorenzo as the rest of us shouted, "I second that!" Lorenzo mumbled, "if that's what y'all want," and didn't speak for the rest of the night.

A plan was hatched. By morning, all six of us at my kitchen table knew what would happen, and what parts we'd play in it. Skylar would stall for time, allowing my father and Gonzalo to prepare the defenses of the farm. Lorenzo would be dispatched to Immokalee and work with the Madariagas. The Madariagas would rally their own troops and the Seminole tribe, and also help us secure additional fuel, weapons and ammo. They would also, my father said, looking sternly at Lorenzo, start working on plans to evacuate the women and children of our family, as well as theirs. "The women and children, if it goes badly. Not us. We fight." Lukas would liaison with veteran militia forces in the area and muster them to Immokalee and the farm. He would also be in charge of arming every worker and peasant capable of fighting, and put all others, young and old, to work the fields, hoping for a harvest in the unlikely case we'd survive to see December.

In the meantime, Skylar would rally all the support she could from her ecoterrorist contacts, and mine Dr. Wu for information about weak spots in Raymond Page's Naples compound. And I would work on a plan to take our fury to the enemy, beheading FloTech and closing the gate to their underworld allies, in what amounted to a suicide mission.

As the others mounted and left at a gallop to start preparing for the trial of their lives, Skylar and I laid in the *hamaca matrimonial*, the double-size hammock, watching the sun rise, sharing the silence.

Thousands were now preparing for war. Messages from Raymond to his Vessel, urging her to leave Immokalee and join him in Naples, got more urgent. Skylar ignored them, spending her time in meditation, steeling herself, gathering her forces.

News from Central Florida improved. Republican troops had for the most part stayed loyal, and spread out all over the territory in guerrilla warfare, so as not to be wiped out by another small nuke. My father Carlos sent word that he'd secure the South for the Republic if Washington could be held back.

Then, on the 20th, one of FloTech's Chinooks, behemoths eighty years old that ran weekly food deliveries from the farm to Naples, appeared on the horizon. This time, it had an escort of two fully armed Apache helicopters and a flotilla of killer drones. I heard it coming in the distance. I closed my eyes and took a deep breath. Then rushed out of my cabin, telling Skylar as I left, "do what I say. Stay hidden here. Don't let the drones see you." I jumped inside my Ranger, which had now been fitted with a .50 machine gun in the back, as she retreated back into the house with Beckenbauer and locked the door. I saw my men running to me and one of Frankie Madariaga's sons, Jesús, approach on his motorcycle. I frantically yelled, "Camilo, in the truck! Jesse, Jesse, follow us!"

We could see the Chinook in the distance, cautiously approaching the helipad by the main warehouse. I saw that my father had put out a decoy, bringing out pallets of food, as if all was normal. After landing, the cargo doors were opened, airmen nervously looking around from inside. I rushed it without thinking, followed by Jesse, as Camilo pointed the .50 to the helicopter. I burst into the cockpit and put my pistol to the head of the pilot: "Do what I say and you live! Turn off the engines!"

The communications system was state-of-the-art, much newer than the airship. I shot an inquiring look to the pilot. "It won't work without my fingerprint." I raised my gun to him and he put his finger to the thumbpad. The screen came to life, with an operator on it. He started talking, but I cut him short: "Shut up! Tell Page this: we have his daughter. Call your escorts, now! She dies if they attack! Understood? Fuck off!"

It worked. The flotilla gained height and disappeared, as my father joined me: "What now?"

"Now, we stall some more. Negotiate. Ask for assurances that our farm will be left alone, offer free elections, whatever. They'll say yes to everything, but we keep demanding guarantees. We drive Page mad. He needs Skylar in eleven days. We can keep him negotiating for maybe a week. He'll run out of patience and lash out at us. If they overrun us in a day, the jig is up, they'll just take Skylar and kill us all. We have to make them pay, maul them, buy time. Then, we start retreating, let him think he's winning. You plead with him to spare the farm, and promise to send Skylar back to him in the Chinook. He won't shoot it down if she's inside. I'll be inside too, and that's as far as my planning goes. I'll be on the ground in Naples, and intend to murder the bastard, so help me God. Skylar will deal with the other stuff, the demons, because nobody else can. You and uncles rally everything we have as we go for the jugular, and mount a counteroffensive to rout and exterminate them."

"Spoken like a true lion, son. Give me a hug."

I went back to Skylar, and we kissed. She was fasting, and seemed to be getting smaller every day. We spent the night saying very little, caressing each other until sleep claimed us. I woke up strangely refreshed considering I had only slept a few hours, with great clarity of mind and feeling strong. Skylar brought me breakfast, and then took one of her devices out of her bag and set it on the table. When I felt ready, she turned it on, and Raymond Page was on the screen. I don't want to talk about him too much, it disgusts me. This was the first time I was seeing his face. He looked like a vampire. Infinitely old and wicked, prying, always prying for a weakness to exploit. He shed crocodile tears for the fate of his "dear baby," whom he asked to see. I pivoted the device slightly for the briefest time, enough for him to see she was there, not enough to try any sort of mind control gimmick.

My father and I kept Page calling to negotiate for a week, until the 27th. He finally realized he'd been played, and launched an attack. Our scouts spotted his troops with enough time to spread out in fields and groves, along creeks, in secret hiding places. Our womenfolk, the very young, and the very old were secreted away. All the peasant families also took cover, and we all left our dwellings behind, for we knew they would be the first to be attacked.

Skylar simply retreated into the citrus grove, sat down, and fell into a deep trance. I left her there as I rushed to meet the invaders.

Drones and helicopters pounded the main farmhouse and other buildings unchallenged. We let them approach to within a certain range, then struck them out of the sky. Drones were caught like fish in nets we had prepared, or blown out of the sky with birdshot. The Apaches didn't have time to gain altitude before being hit by camouflaged nests of machine guns and RPGs.

Distant shots towards the south told us that the Madariagas were already fighting the ground forces in the woods around Immokalee. Soon, gunfire erupted in the north, too: those were our own troops. I went to them in the Ford. As I approached the front line, Florida War veterans came out of their hiding places to salute me with raised fists. My father's command post was set up under an old oak covered in Spanish moss. He was dispatching couriers. "All good at the farm?"

"Good. Those birds are down. How's here?"

"They have some top troops, but not too many, west and north. They brought lots of compound sec, mall cops fat and soft: filler. I have Gonzalo with our best veterans holding their strongest column, Screaming Eagles. Our *campesinos* are picking the mall cops off one by one with rifles and machetes."

"The Madariagas?"

"Frankie says they've got it. They're holding and not letting anybody get close to Immokalee and the back of the farm."

"That's good, Pa. Give them hell for a day or two, then start falling back."

A short Indian man in *huaraches*, tire-rubber sandals, approached us running. My father took him aside and came back to me grim-faced: "You won't like this. Frankie says they sent a party to Ponce de León and burned it to the ground. Some had taken refuge there and were massacred. Ms. Gonzalez too, son. I'm sorry."

"*Que hijos de puta. Que hijos de una gran puta* ... I'll take Camilo and some troops and hit them on their way out."

"Don't. We need you to cut the snake's head."

"I'll be fine, Pa. Just hit them hard and pull back. It's the plan anyway."

I jumped back into the truck before he could say anything, and drove off with another couple of truck-mounted .50s following. We took backroads and shortcuts, firing bursts and scattering enemy troops when we spotted them, but not stopping until we arrived in the glare of Ponce's buildings burning. We slowly drove around until reaching the demo garden. I got off the truck and approached the bullet-riddled corpse of Ms. Gonzalez lying in a pool of blood by a bed of newly sprouted carrots. She had the machete she used to cut and strip bamboo stakes still clutched in her hand, and her open eyes pierced the darkening sky above her. Crying, I knelt and closed them. "You are now in the *milpa* with your *hermanita*. I'll see you there. Rest." Then I heard laughs, and the sound of clinking bottles. I signaled my men to dismount and approach the sound quietly. We saw a group of maybe thirty troops in compound security uniforms laughing and drinking around a bonfire. They were all that had been needed to raid the university grounds, full of civilians. Camilo signaled to silently spread around in the palmetto and wait for my lead. I aimed and shot a fat man with ribbons in his uniform with my pistol, then kept shooting as my men fired too, and soon they were all down. The last few had raised their arms in surrender, and been shot anyway, for that's war. Some had fallen into the bonfire and it started smelling of roast meat as we walked around the bodies taking their weapons and ammo, and shooting the wounded in the head.

12

Skylar was still in the lotus position in the orange grove, her eyes closed, barely breathing. I came back to check on her often. She wouldn't wake up or speak to me. Only Beckenbauer guarded her, lying at her feet day and night as the Bohns and the Madariagas played cat-and-mouse with the invaders, killing and dying, slowly retreating. The morning of the 30th I heard Skylar's device vibrate. I picked it up, took a deep breath, and accepted Page's call. His face was contorted in fury, and before a word was exchanged, he picked the severed head of my uncle Lorenzo, grabbing it by an ear, shoving it to an inch of his camera lens. "See this worm? See him, beaner? He thought he could make a deal with me. He thought he'd get something from me. He wanted out, and ha! out he is! He also wanted out for your women, you filthy beaner, and for the women and brats of all the other fucking beaners and Mexicans, and I'll let them out, too. One by one, starting now!" As he said that, a young, Indian-faced girl was dragged into the field of vision by a uniformed thug. One of Frankie Madariaga's granddaughters. Unceremoniously, Raymond Page stood up, pulled a knife and slit her throat. As the goon let her fall, he approached the camera again and thundered: "I'll do the same to all of them, every ten minutes, until my daughter is back with me! Understand! Then I'll go there and do the same to every living thing in and around Immokalee! With them!" He swiveled the camera to focus on another screen. It showed black-clad, exoskeleton-wearing, powerfully armed Washington troops and battle robots entering Naples. "Understand! We've won already! Give her up, or be exterminated, every last one of you!"

Skylar spoke to the screen. She had been standing behind me for a while. "Yes, Father. I will go back in the big helicopter now. Your command will be obeyed." I turned off the screen and faced her. She smiled faintly and said, "It's now, love. Before he gets the new troops, before he kills too many of those poor folk. Let's go."

The Chinook's engines were roaring when we arrived, Skylar, myself and Beckenbauer in the back of the truck. My choicest troops were in its belly, and the pilot sweated under the helmet as I sat next to him, prodded his ribs with my Glock, and said, "Fly us to FloTech compound. Try anything, any code message, anything, and I'll shoot you and toss you out of the cockpit like trash. Go."

The great beast took to the air. I looked into its cargo area and saw the hard, stoic faces of my clan's warriors, and very small among them, Skylar, slowly starting to glow. A soft glow faintly surrounded her as her hour of doom approached. The men cast respectful glances in her direction and clutched their weapons. "Initiating descent, sir," the pilot said after a while, and Skylar's voice rose over the roar of the engines, "Not yet! Fly above the South Lab first!" I nodded to the pilot to do as she had said, and looked into her eyes. She spoke to me without moving her lips. Her voice was sweet inside my head as she told me, "That's where the gate is, love. The mouth. Where I need to push the demon into. Kill that man, don't let him take me. And if you can't kill him, kill me, kill me before tomorrow, for I don't want to be his Vessel." And as everybody gasped she slid one of the cargo doors open and stepped outside. Into the air. Beckenbauer almost jumped outside to follow her too, but I grabbed him at the last second.

The helicopter continued its half-circle course towards the main helipad, which was atop the biggest building in town, right on the beach off of Vanderbilt Road, FloTech's corporate headquarters and Mr. Page's own residence as well. We all looked out of the windows of the Chinook, and when the angle was right to see the spot where she had jumped off again, a marvelous vision was revealed: Skylar was floating in the air hundreds of feet above the South Lab, getting smaller and smaller as we flew away, becoming a point of bright, blinding light. Suddenly her voice exploded in the sky, shattering the glass of windows in the Lab. It was her voice, and at the same time it wasn't, it was like an angry angel's, like a hurricane, sibilant and powerful, uttering ... what? What curses, what invocations, what spells? For that's what it was, I knew without understanding a word of it, a weapon, not a voice. As her litany continued, I could see walls collapsing. I had the impression of another luminous figure, on the ground, small in the distance but almost as bright as Skylar, a man with a staff walking towards the crumbling lab building, casting angry invocations as well, in a much lower key. "Ah, Dr. Wu," I thought, "you have to close what you helped open. Don't let Skylar do it alone." Then, I couldn't look anymore, because we were in the last meters of air above the rooftop helipad, ready to touch down. A heavily armed platoon had their weapons pointed towards us, and in their midst ... could that be ... was that my target? "Turn on facial recog, now!" I screamed to the pilot. "I'm trying to land this thing, goddammit!" "Hover right here, turn facial on and point it to that man in a suit right there, or you die!" He jerked the controls to stop the descent, and as the wind from the rotor blades forced the men on the roof to scatter and grab onto rails, he held the stick with one hand as he operated a screen with the other. The image was blurry, then the camera adjusted, moved out of focus again and finally, for a second, I saw him. I knew it before the voice system said "Raymond Page. FloTechCorp CEO. Technology Party candidate. Philanthropist and ..."

I tried to open the window on the co-pilot side but couldn't. So I shot it, then kicked the shattered plexiglass to make an opening big enough to let half of my body out, pistol in hand. My ears were exploding with the fearsome invocations that pierced the air, and with a wailing, otherworldy cry that seemed to emerge from the disintegrating South Lab, as I emptied the magazine. I hit the bastard at least once, but he ducked and started crawling away—in a second, he had understood what was going on near the Lab, had understood his Vessel wasn't on the Chinook, and in pain and fury was ordering his troops to open fire on us. Time slowed for me as I managed to get back inside the cockpit, tracers heading towards us as his troops on the roof discharged a wall of fire that started hitting the machine like hail. "Pilot, land us now!" I screamed, but the large airship kept veering sideways—soon the helipad would not be below us anymore, but 160 stories of air, and we couldn't levitate like Skylar. "Pilot!" I screamed again, then saw he was dead. Grab the stick and try to control the Chinook, or jump out now, while we still could? "Out, out, out, out!" I yelled, and the men started jumping out through the cargo doors, into chaos and bullets. *"Beckenbauer! Folge mir!"* I screamed as I jumped, with only a few inches of roof left under us, and the noble beast followed with a great leap. He hit the ground running and took another giant leap that landed him right upon Raymond Page, who was trying to reach the stairs door, trailing blood. Beckenbauer's jaws closed on the fiend's neck, and I ran towards them, sensing rather than seeing the infernal scene all around me as farm militia battled the guard. The Chinook's rotors hit the side of the building on the way down, until it veered off some and ended crashing on the Waterside Mall below and bursting into a ball of fire. The fever pitch of the spells and the piercing howling and wailing that answered them some distance away continued. I couldn't stop for a second to make sense of it all. All I could see was my loyal Becks holding my enemy for me, helping me kill it. I had two bullets come through me at that point, and had broken a foot upon landing, but didn't feel any pain. Enraged, I saw that Page had a knife in his hand, the same one he had used to murder Madariaga's grandchild, and was furiously stabbing my dog with it, who nevertheless would not let go. His teeth were buried deep in Page's neck even in death. A last spark of life animated Raymond Page's hand, which kept weakly stabbing my dead dog. Slowly, almost gently, I took the bloody knife from his hand. With a great effort, I pushed poor dead Beckenbauer to the side. *"Alles is gut, mein Freund. Danke, Freund, vielen dank. Wiedersehen, Beck".* Then I looked at the wretch laying there in a pool of his own, and my dog's, blood. His makeup was a mess, as tears streamed down his cheeks. His wig had moved to one side, and the stench was unmistakable: he had soiled himself. Then he, the last scion of a long line of wizards, the man who would drink the blood and life energy of countless victims, who fancied himself the first superman, pleaded for his life. Begged for his life in the most disgraceful, humiliating way, promising power and riches if only ... if only ... I didn't let him finish, and slit his throat from side to side, slicing deep with a serrating motion as if butchering a hog back at the farm, almost cutting his head off.

    The rooftop battle was over. FloTech's fighters were all dead, and most of the farm militia too. Old Camilo, badly wounded, came to me, and we helped each other crawl to the edge to witness the battle around the lab. A giant, darkened crater marked the spot where Dr. Wu had stood, aiding Skylar with his own spells. The lab was in ruins, revealing the entrance of a dark, huge cave underneath. An enormous wraith, a shape that in turn looked like a giant bat, a snake, or a machine, shrieked and wailed as a tiny figure, Skylar, now on the ground, both hands raised, walked and seemed to push it towards that cave entrance with every tempest of sound she coaxed her tiny body to utter. Step by step she drove it back, and the monster writhed and recoiled, viciously lashing out with a tail, a claw, a string of curses deep and powerful that hit my beloved and almost felled her. But she gathered what strength she still had and kept pushing, relentlessly pushing, the god into the hole.

"Camilo, the stairs! Let's help her! *Vamos!*"

Before we could move, her voice filled my skull. Her sweet voice that I adored, I heard for the last time. "You live, my love. You plant more seeds, and teach others to live free of hubris in this world, not seeking to be Gaia's masters but her servants, and to leave the old demons alone, rejecting the power they offer. Let them eat mice and birds, not souls. Tell the humans to stay few, for Gaia cannot feed many. I will not be a Vessel, thanks to you. Thank you for our time together, and for your courage. *Adiós*, Rodrigo."

Then she charged the Naples God with the last of her strength and fury, pushing him to the pit in the ground, into which they fell together. I tried to scream but nothing came out of my throat. "*¡Don Rodrigo! Mire, don Rodrigo,*" Camilo said, pointing east, to Immokalee, and I saw a mighty explosion rising, a mushroom cloud. "All is lost," I thought, and fell into darkness.

I came to myself feeling sick. My wounds ached terribly, and the world rocked back and forth. Slowly, I realized I was in a cabin, on a boat. Camilo was looking at me, his arm in a sling, with another man I didn't know. "Skylar! Father, uncles, brother ... where?" I managed to say. "Don't think of that, don Rodrigo," he answered, "This man here is don Gorostiza, the captain. A larger boat is waiting in La Habana. We, and the others we were able to save, will then travel to Buenos Aires, to the other Bohns. Frankie Madariaga made sure of that. Now rest."

They say a cult of Skylar has been growing in Florida since I left, fought by the powers that be but spreading like wildfire nevertheless. The humblest laborers and slaves, freed of the unknown god buried by Skylar, albeit still living harsh, desperate lives under purely human masters, whisper her name and secretly get her symbol tattooed at night, in barns and groves: a smiling woman's face with three eyes, hair growing into tree branches, under a moon, an owl and a bee. I am alive to witness the first stages of the woman I loved becoming a goddess.

Contributors

Nathan Beebe Peltier (cover art) is a visual artist raised in Minnesota. He studied Geology at Northland College in Wisconsin, and Ecological Design and Architecture at ECOSA Institute in Arizona. Lake Superior and the high desert have informed him and his work. Nathan currently works primarily with ink and digital mediums, but has been known for tattooing, electroformed jewelry, and block printing. He is inspired by architecture, dreams, love, and the apocalypse.

Justin Patrick Moore's work has appeared in *Mythic: A Quarterly Science Fiction and Fantasy Magazine*, *Love in the Ruins: Tales of Romance in the Deindustrial Future*, and *Abraxas: International Journal of Esoteric Studies*. His essays on culture, subculture and a variety of other subjects appear frequently on his website sothismedias.com. He is also an avid radio hobbyist. Justin and his wife Audrey make their home in Cincinnati, the Queen of the West.

Yvonne Rowse has been a reader of science fiction for a long time, with a preference for survivable apocalypses. Recently her interests have widened to include post-industrial stories, preferably with likeable protagonists, and an examination of the societies that develop following a loss of technology. She has retired from an environmental management career that never seemed to improve environmental outcomes and now lives in Derbyshire in the UK, dreaming about taking trains to Italy (outside of the growing season).

Tom Murphy is a professor of physics at UC San Diego. An undergraduate at Georgia Tech and graduate student at Caltech, Prof. Murphy has spent a career pushing the boundaries of astrophysical instrumentation and science. Along the way, he has developed a growing interest in societal energy, experimenting with off-grid solar and storage technologies on the side. In 2021, Prof. Murphy published an open-access general-education textbook called *Energy and Human Ambitions on a Finite Planet*, available in PDF form to anyone.

Daniel Crawford studied in the salt-mines of Lit Crit for some years, and has always liked stories that are held together by metaphor and symbolism as much as by conventional plot and character. A Magical Realist story is ideal for this, and, just as all the names of the characters here have significance, so the unstated mystical sub-text of the story can be deduced from many small allusions. The idea of trying to write a story combining speculative finance, greed, violence, and stupidity with a mystical subtext, once it appeared, wouldn't go away. Given this opportunity, he wrote it down.

Eric Rust Backos lives in Lake County, Ohio where he practices Druidry and Green Wizardry. The setting and characters started as idea for an adventure module for John Greer's RPG *Weird of Hali: Roleplaying the Other Side of the Cthulhu Mythos*, but Maple County is in a different universe. Thanks to John for his help developing the occult slide rule. *Baie dankie* to fellow rugby player Marcu Knoesen for Afrikaans lessons and for inventing a handful of occult titles in that language.

G. Kay Bishop was born in the rain-shadow of ancient hills whence the gourd and the squash originated and dwells within holler of the high, lonesome sounds echoing from hills taller and a tad younger where traces of Elizabethan diction still linger. The soundtrack for this lifetime has old-timey music in the background, sprightly Renaissance dance in the foreground, and odd pop-up stanzas of "It's a Long Way from Amphioxus" punctuated by crabbed mutterings about people who WILL not learn to distinguish "it's" from "its" and use "I" as the object of prepositions—thinking it is polite, when it is just ear-scraping and ungrammatical. Let the music of language be ever tuneable and sound.

Santiago De Choch spent his youth traveling and doing odd jobs in many parts of the world. Many of those were in agriculture. There is a strong spiritual element in the relationship between man and his food that's still present in some regions. Others have lost it. From the potato harvest in the high Andes of Bolivia to avocado culture in Israel and the vast produce fields of Florida, many experiences went into this tale. He lives and farms in Suwannee County, Fla., and can be reached at seedandpen@gmail.com.

Nathanael Bonnell grew up in turn-of-the-millennium Cincinnati and, after a long series of vagabonding adventures and misadventures, now lives with his partner Misty and baby son Ivor in Wisconsin's northwoods, where he wears hats from a steadily expanding collection, including "editor," "landscaper," "farmhand," and, most recently, "signpainter." He hopes to finish making a nice hewn-log shave horse soon so he and Misty can use it to build a yurt.

Comments for contributors sent to the editor will be forwarded.

COLOPHON

New Maps is typeset by the editor using an ancient, temperamental program called LaTeX which nevertheless produces unsurpassable results. The text font is an early digital version of Hermann Zapf's Palatino—resurrected from abandoned files and fitted with modern amenities like kerning tables and characters like Þ—which retains all the calligraphic warmth of the 1950s original cut that was lost in the production of the popular Linotype version. Titles are set in Sebastian Nagel's 2010 typeface Tierra Nueva, which is based on lettering from a 1562 map of the Americas; headers, drop caps, and miscellany are in Warren Chappell's classic Lydian; monospace text uses Spline Mono.

ACKNOWLEDGMENTS

Thanks to Megan Katherine, Greg Moffitt, and Frank Kaminski, as well as to all the people I run into who believe in this project right away. And, as ever, my deepest thanks to Misty for keeping the homestead running on those mornings after I've been up late assembling the magazine.

Printed in Great Britain
by Amazon